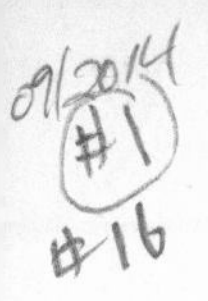

Gérard de Villiers

THE MADMEN OF BENGHAZI

Gérard de Villiers (1929–2013) is the most popular spy-thriller writer in French history. His hundred-odd books about the adventures of the Austrian nobleman and freelance CIA operative Malko Linge have sold millions of copies.

Malko Linge, who first appeared in 1964, has often been compared to Ian Fleming's hero James Bond. The two secret agents share a taste for gunplay and kinky sex, but de Villiers was a journalist at heart, and his books are based on constant travel and reporting in dozens of countries.

On several occasions de Villiers was even ahead of the news. His 1980 novel had Islamists killing President Anwar el-Sādāt of Egypt a year before the event took place. *The Madmen of Benghazi* and *Chaos in Kabul* vividly reflect the current upheaval in Libya and Afghanistan.

THE MADMEN OF BENGHAZI

THE MADMEN OF BENGHAZI

Gérard de Villiers

Translated from the French by William Rodarmor

Vintage Canada

VINTAGE CANADA EDITION, 2014

Published in Canada by Vintage Canada, a division of Random House of Canada Limited, Toronto, in 2014, and simultaneously in the United States by Vintage Books, a division of Random House LLC, New York, a Penguin Random House company. Originally published in France as *Les Fous de Benghazi* by Éditions Gérard de Villiers, Paris, in 2011. Distributed in Canada by Random House of Canada Limited.

www.randomhouse.ca

Library and Archives Canada Cataloguing in Publication

Villiers, Gérard de, 1929–2013
[Fous de Benghazi. English]

The madmen of Benghazi / by Gérard de Villiers ; translated from the French by William Rodarmor.

(The Malko series)
Translation of: Les fous de Benghazi.

Issued in print and electronic formats.

ISBN 978-0-345-80817-2

I. Rodarmor, William, translator II. Title. III. Title: Fous de Benghazi. English

PQ2682.I44F6813 2014 843'.914 C2014-902808-3

Book design by Joy O'Meara

Printed and bound in the United States of America

2 4 6 8 9 7 5 3 1

THE MADMEN OF BENGHAZI

CHAPTER 1

Ibrahim al-Senussi was stark naked when he stepped out of the shower, and he stopped dead at his bedroom door. Cynthia was sitting on the edge of the big bed, making a call on her cell phone. That wasn't sexy in itself, but between the lapels of the young woman's Chanel suit—his birthday present to her—he could see her nipples straining against the raw-silk blouse.

Cynthia's shapely legs were bare from her upper thigh to her tawny, very high-heeled boots. The length of her skirt had once been quite proper—until she had the hem raised.

Al-Senussi felt the blood rushing to his crotch.

It had taken him months to get Cynthia Mulligan into bed. When he first met her, the thirtyish blonde was so gorgeous it made his head spin. She was wearing a practically transparent blue muslin Dior dress that set off her slim body and long legs to their best advantage.

She didn't seem standoffish, either. When al-Senussi smilingly approached, she'd been happy to chat. And he didn't have too much trouble persuading her to have dinner with him at Annabel's, one of the few places in London that still served decent caviar. Between glasses of champagne, they took a spin on the small dance floor.

Al-Senussi wanted to pull her close, but Cynthia modestly kept her distance. Still, her almond-shaped eyes hardly looked shy. He forced himself to be patient, figuring she might not like public displays of affection.

For the Libyan, disappointment came at midnight.

"I have to go home," Cynthia said with an apologetic smile. "I'm getting up at seven tomorrow."

"But why?" he stammered.

"I'm working. I have a shoot for *Vogue* at eight thirty in the morning."

A top fashion model, Cynthia Mulligan had a job that involved tricky schedules and lots of travel.

Feeling aggrieved, al-Senussi took her back to her apartment on Mulberry Walk in Chelsea. They parted with a kiss that was almost chaste, though it let him taste Cynthia's lips and feverishly brush one of her full breasts.

Alas, after that semi-exquisite evening, he didn't see her again for another two months. And not for want of trying.

He invited her to Monte Carlo for the Rose Ball; to Marbella for a dream weekend on a friend's boat—he would fetch her by helicopter from Málaga Airport, he said, and fly her directly to a two-hundred-foot yacht moored at Puerto Banús; to Venice for a private tour of François Pinault's collection; to Paris and an ultra-luxurious suite at the Four Seasons.

Each time, Cynthia turned him down for the same reason: her work.

And then one day when they were having a drink at the Dorchester, she mentioned that her birthday was coming up. He seized the opportunity to ask her out, half threatening, half pleading.

Miraculously, the cover girl agreed: for dinner, again at Annabel's.

On the day, al-Senussi had a three-thousand-pound Chanel suit delivered to her—when you're in love, you don't pinch pennies. But when he came to pick her up, he felt a pang of disappointment: she wasn't wearing the suit. Instead she had on the dress she'd worn when they first met, but she had now put on black stockings—a look that always set his pulse racing.

The dinner went off without a hitch. When it was over, al-Senussi said:

"I have champagne and a birthday cake waiting at my place."

Heart pounding, he expected to be rebuffed. Instead, she smiled and said:

"That sounds nice."

With Cynthia, al-Senussi always felt he was walking on eggshells, and by the time his Bentley pulled up at his Belgravia house, he was practically having a heart attack. As they entered the apartment she asked for a glass of water, and he ran to the kitchen to get it. When he came back, the young woman had lit the three candles arranged on the table.

He brought out a bottle of Roederer Cristal and popped the cork.

They drank a toast.

"Happy birthday, darling," he murmured.

Their lips met and he slipped his arm firmly around Cynthia's waist. Unmoved at first, the young woman then returned his kiss. She pulled back so their tongues could touch in the air, which she seemed to find more exciting.

This playful caprice sparked a frenzy of desire in al-Senussi.

His hands ran all over her body, caressing, squeezing, and exploring her like he was a high schooler in heat. When his fingers brushed the silky fabric of her panties, he yanked on the lace so hard that it ripped.

Her clothes in disarray, and leaning against the dining table, Cynthia seemed to enjoy this sexual tornado.

Encouraged by her silent acceptance, al-Senussi loosened his clothes, freeing his unusually long cock.

With an elegance that showed her good breeding, Cynthia gently took hold of it.

Frowning fiercely, al-Senussi couldn't control himself any longer. Before they even reached the bedroom, he tipped Cynthia onto a black velvet sofa, knelt in front of her on the carpet, and jammed his cock in.

"Go easy, love," she said softly, her legs now raised against her new lover's shoulders. "You're very big."

Al-Senussi ignored her, focusing his attention on his energetic thrusting. He came with a yell and collapsed like a marathon runner crossing the finish line.

Cynthia gently stroked his curly head.

"You must have wanted me very badly," she said affectionately.

"I've been wanting you for months!"

Cynthia shifted slightly to make herself more comfortable.

"You aren't leaving, are you?" he exclaimed anxiously.

"How could I?" she asked with a mischievous smile. "You ripped my knickers. I can't go home without any underwear."

Al-Senussi discovered that Cynthia was an expert at all sorts of erotic games, if a somewhat detached player. With that evening, their relationship really began. Cynthia refused to move into his house, but they saw each other often and went on weekend trips together.

For al-Senussi, it was a period of pure happiness.

Just the same, he'd pondered long and hard before suggesting that she come with him to Cairo.

"Why Cairo?" she asked, wide-eyed.

Taking the plunge, he decided to reveal a hidden aspect of his life.

"I have to tell you a secret," he said. "I'm the grandson of King Idris of Libya, the one Muammar Qaddafi overthrew in 1967. Some people want me to be the head of the new Libya, once we're rid of him."

Cynthia wasn't especially interested in the vagaries of the Arab world, but she always tried to be polite.

"What people?" she asked.

"I can't tell you yet."

"Why do you have to go to Cairo?"

"To meet with some Libyans who will support the new government. To talk about the future."

"Will you be there long?"

"A couple of weeks."

"Then I'll see you when you come back. I don't feel like going to Egypt."

At that point, al-Senussi fell to his knees, ready to do anything to get her to go with him. He rattled on about the Pyramids, the pharaohs, Cairo's perfect climate, and the charms of the huge metropolis.

In fact, he mainly wanted to exhaust himself on Cynthia's magnificent body.

It took two days of repeated phone calls and a Bulgari wristwatch to persuade Cynthia to accompany him, but she eventually showed up at his apartment with an elegant Vuitton suitcase. The weather in London had been especially foul that week, which may have played a role in her decision.

"Aren't you getting dressed?" Cynthia asked coolly, having ended her phone conversation.

Al-Senussi was still standing in front of her, buck naked.

"You're looking very beautiful!" he muttered in a strangled voice.

She casually parted her knees, briefly revealing a flash of white underwear.

Though almost certainly innocent, this was the drop that made the bucket overflow. Staring, al-Senussi grabbed her wrist and pulled her to her feet. Their bodies were almost touching. He slipped a hand under the Chanel skirt, reached the young woman's stomach, and grabbed her nylon panties.

"One for the road!" he growled.

He was already pulling them down when the intercom buzzed. The sound was about as welcome as the klaxon of a diving submarine.

Furious, he grunted and ran to the front door.

"A gentleman is waiting to take you to the airport, sir," the building's concierge announced smoothly. "He says there's not a minute to lose, because traffic is very bad toward Heathrow. I'll put him on the line."

An equally smooth, but much firmer, voice now came on.

It was Scott Ridley.

"Ibrahim, you have to be downstairs in five minutes or you'll miss your plane."

He opened his mouth, about to protest—after all, he might be the future king of Libya—but yielded.

Scott Ridley, the MI6 agent who was his handler, inspired in al-Senussi a kind of fearful respect. Always impeccably dressed, with his calm voice and cold eyes, the man was as smooth as a stone.

"Okay, I'll be right down. I just got out of the shower."

It was five p.m. as the last passengers for Cairo filed aboard British Airways Flight 132. The Boeing 777 was nearly full except in first class, which Cynthia Mulligan and Ibrahim al-Senussi had to themselves.

Takeoff from Heathrow was scheduled for 5:15, and the doors were closing.

"Who were those people who took us to the airport?" asked Cynthia when they were seated. "And how did they get us through immigration and customs ahead of everyone?"

"They're police officers," said al-Senussi. "My protection detail. With what's happening in Libya, I've become someone—an important person."

"What about the man in charge? You know, the one who looked like he was modeling for Burberry?"

Al-Senussi mumbled something about a chief inspector, and Cynthia seemed satisfied.

In fact, the man in the well-cut trench coat was with neither Burberry nor the police. Scott Ridley was the MI6 officer who had first suggested a new future for the Libyan prince.

The 777 pulled back from the Jetway and headed for the tarmac. A few moments later, as the plane prepared for takeoff, a cabin attendant made an announcement:

"Our next stop will be Cairo, where we are due to arrive at 10:55 p.m. local time. You will be served a meal shortly after takeoff."

Outside, darkness had already fallen on London.

Al-Senussi spread a blanket across his lap, then took Cynthia's hand and put it on his crotch.

She gave his swelling erection a squeeze through his pants, and smiled.

"You're insatiable!" she whispered.

The idea of sex in flight appealed to her. She'd had her first orgasm while masturbating to an erotic scene from *Emmanuelle* set on an airplane.

Shielded by the blanket, she playfully began to stroke al-Senussi's prick. Her delighted lover leaned back, his eyes closed. He opened them only when the flight attendant reached over to unlock his tray table for dinner.

"We aren't hungry!" he hissed.

The young woman didn't insist, and instead dimmed the cabin lights and went to sit down. The 777 had reached its cruising altitude and was flying smoothly at thirty-six thousand feet. Aside from the rumble of its twin jets, the silence was total.

Al-Senussi pulled his zipper down, and his cock popped up like a jack-in-the-box. Cynthia glanced back at the stewardess. The woman seemed to be dozing, so she pushed the blanket aside and bent to take al-Senussi in her mouth. Now feeling very excited herself, she started energetically masturbating as she sucked al-Senussi off. Her mouth was dancing a wild ballet on his prick, and he was gasping. By now, he knew how skilled Cynthia was at blow jobs, but each time was a dazzling revelation.

Yielding to her incomparable mastery, he came, stifling a groan and arching his back in the seat.

Alerted by the sound, the flight attendant looked over just as Cynthia raised her head to reveal a still-erect penis—and give the woman a tingling in her own groin.

Now at peace, al-Senussi kissed Cynthia's hand.

"It's going to be great in Cairo," he murmured.

The gray van took El Aruba Avenue as it circled Cairo Airport to the south. A fourteen-foot cyclone fence punctuated with watchtowers ran along the road, with concrete sentry boxes housing drowsy soldiers with AK-47s. Egypt wasn't at war, but it wasn't exactly at peace.

The van reached the end of the avenue and turned onto the frontage road along the airport perimeter. It drove another hundred yards, then slowed and stopped just as a Boeing 737 passed overhead on final approach. The end of the main runway was barely three hundred yards from the fence.

The moment the van stopped, its driver jumped out and raised its hood, as if it had broken down. Stopping on the roads around the airport was forbidden, and a breakdown would give him cover. He climbed back in and dialed a number on his cell phone.

It was 10:45 p.m.

Inside the van, it was deathly quiet. Two men dressed European style in shirts and jeans were seated on either side of a stepladder that provided access to a hatch in the roof.

From time to time, they looked at their watches. The minutes ticked by slowly. At 10:50 p.m., one leaned forward and asked the driver in Arabic:

"See anything yet?"

"No," he answered, keeping his eyes on the part of the sky where the planes on final approach appeared. At night, their powerful landing lights made them easy to spot. That wasn't enough to identify them, of course, but when they passed three hundred feet above the frontage road, it was easy to make out the airline logos.

Since the van stopped, three planes had landed: two Egyptian and one Saudi.

Silence fell again.

Abdul Gabal al-Afghani, the oldest of the three men, kept staring at his watch, his stomach tense.

It was exactly 10:55 p.m.

The van driver was watching both his rearview mirror and the sky to his left. Police cars occasionally patrolled the airport, and if one came by now, it was sure to be suspicious of them.

Ten more minutes passed in leaden silence. The driver swiveled around and hissed:

"Five more minutes, and we're leaving."

Two minutes passed, with the three men praying to God with all their might.

Suddenly a yelp came from the cabin.

"Inshallah, I think that's it!"

He had spotted the landing lights of a passenger plane that would pass over them as it came in to land.

Al-Afghani raced up the stepladder, opened the hatch, and slid onto the van's roof.

Now he could see the white lights in the sky to his left. In another minute or two, the plane would be overhead. The other man in the van passed al-Afghani a long metal tube. He picked it up and rested it on his shoulder. It was a SAM-14 Strela missile launcher. The Russian-made surface-to-air missile had an infrared guidance system on a gyroscopic platform. A formidable weapon, it weighed only twenty-three pounds and could be fired by a single man.

The airliner's landing lights were now very close. According to the schedule, it should be British Airways Flight 132. Even throttled back, its twin jets' thunder was deafening.

Standing on the roof of the van, al-Afghani pivoted to his left. He had just moments to act.

Holding his breath, he kept his eye on the plane, slowly turning as it approached. The big airliner passed about three hundred feet above the ground, and he recognized the British Airways logo on its tail.

It was his target.

The plane was now right in front of him, descending toward the runway, the glow of its two jets clearly visible.

It would touch down in about thirty seconds. Al-Afghani activated the target-seeking system, and a buzzer and a blinking red light told him that the Strela had locked onto its target. To send the missile streaking toward the plane, all he had to do was pull the trigger.

The captain of the 777 had switched off the automatic pilot and was concentrating on his instruments as he brought the plane in for landing. Suddenly, his copilot screamed:

"Oh my God!"

The pilot jerked his head up, catching a momentary glimpse

of a man standing on a van by the airport fence, pointing a long tube at his plane.

Of all possible dangers, this was the absolute worst: a missile fired at a passenger plane, which was as vulnerable as an elephant before a tank.

Clutching the controls, the pilot yelled into his microphone:

"Cairo Control, terrorist attack! Terrorist attack! BA 132! BA 132!"

Knowing that it wouldn't do any good.

Al-Afghani held his breath and pulled the Strela's trigger. In front of him, the huge bulk of the Boeing 777 was still a hundred feet off the ground. The launcher gave a muffled thump, and its recoil knocked him backward. The missile raced straight for the plane at nine thousand miles per hour, its infrared guidance system locked onto the heat of the two jet engines.

Without waiting to see the result of his shot, al-Afghani jumped down inside the van, threw the launcher into the back, and yelled:

"*Allahu akbar!*"

The driver had already started up the engine, and he made a fast U-turn back toward the Airport Bridge and Ahmed Ismail Boulevard, the road leading to Cairo.

The Mercedes carrying Malko Linge turned off the Nile Road and stopped at a row of retractable bollards protecting the entrance of the Four Seasons Hotel.

A guard flipped a switch, the bollards sank into the roadway, and the Mercedes drove on to the hotel entrance. The Four Seasons overlooked the Nile, and its soaring columns suggested the Egypt of the pharaohs. The neighborhood was called Garden City, but there wasn't a scrap of greenery to be seen.

Cairo was one of the ugliest cities in the world, Malko thought. The facades of the buildings along the Nile were black and grimy, pockmarked by countless air conditioners. Coming in from the airport, all the Austrian saw were endless blocks of tan, twenty-story buildings, with hundreds of dish antennas sprouting from their flat roofs. The flat, sprawling, scabby city reminded him of the Soviet Union.

At the last census, Cairo had eighteen million inhabitants, a quarter of the entire Egyptian population. Aside from the tourist hotels on the banks of the Nile, it was a jumble of decaying apartment houses jammed one next to the other. A tangle of urban freeways made the city especially unpleasant, not to mention traffic that clogged the streets for miles.

Malko's car had spent ten minutes stuck behind a Volkswagen minibus full of women in *niqabs* that had broken down in the middle of the road.

As he got out of the Mercedes, his driver respectfully said:

"I'll wait for you here, sir."

The driver was a powerfully built man with huge eyebrows, a thick mustache, and a square jaw who'd met Malko at the airport terminal. He said his name was Nasser Ihab, and he'd been sent by the American embassy. What he didn't tell Malko until later was that he was an agent of the Mukhabarat, Egypt's domestic intelligence service.

Malko entered the hotel's majestic lobby. In the center of the marble floor stood a raised tearoom occupied only by men. Below them, a pianist played melancholy tunes reminiscent of a hotel in Eastern Europe.

Registration was handled in record time by a smiling desk clerk. There were almost no tourists in Egypt these days, and the staff was especially affable.

Within minutes, Malko was in a beautiful room overlooking the brown waters of the Nile. Thanks to air-conditioning, the place was pleasantly chilly. He took a quick shower and went back downstairs to the Mercedes. He dropped into the backseat, and Nasser took off immediately.

"We're going to the American embassy," Malko announced.

They passed the large British diplomatic compound, which

ran along a hundred yards of riverfront, then left the Nile for the narrow streets of Saadan City.

Once again, Malko found himself in a new country without quite knowing why.

In a friendly phone call, the CIA station chief in Vienna had asked him if he wouldn't mind going to Cairo for the Agency. Without telling him why, of course.

It would have been hard for Malko to refuse. Winter was approaching and the bills to maintain his beloved Liezen castle would soon come flooding in. If it weren't for his freelance CIA work, Malko would be just another impoverished Austrian noble-man, probably renting out his ancestral home for business retreats. But Malko had some highly specialized talents that the CIA employed on a regular basis. The Agency paid top dollar, but in exchange gave him the riskiest assignments.

Malko had invited his longtime fiancée, Alexandra, to come to Egypt with him, but she politely refused. The Upper Austria social season was about to begin and she didn't want to miss any of the galas. Her one concession to Malko: dressed in a bustier and smoky gray tights, she concocted a particularly erotic farewell dinner, and afterward gave him a dazzling demonstration of her talents, as if to show him what he was leaving behind. The next day she agreed to accompany him to Schwechat airport for a quickie on the road, having taken the elementary precaution of not wearing panties.

Nasser stopped the Mercedes at a little square five hundred yards beyond the British embassy. He turned back to Malko and pointed to a street on the left.

"Amerika-el-Latiniya is closed off," he said. "There's no way to drive any farther. The embassy's just a hundred yards away. Here's my number. Call me when you're finished."

By then, a nervous traffic cop was already waving him on.

The Cairene police were on edge. After a recent incident in the Sinai, where Israeli border guards had killed five Egyptian policemen, the crowd peacefully demonstrating in Tahrir Square had stormed the Israeli embassy. It occupied the top three floors in the Shana al-Tahrir building between Nadar Square and the El-Gamaa Bridge on the west bank of the Nile.

With contagious enthusiasm, hundreds of young people attacked the place, even though it was protected by the army. They didn't set the building on fire—most of the other tenants were Egyptian—just smashed in the embassy office doors. The Israelis barricaded themselves on the top two floors and called for help. Frustrated in their desire to throw the diplomats out the window, the mob tossed their files out instead.

A demonstrator tore down the Israeli flag hanging on the facade and replaced it with an Egyptian one.

A police helicopter landed on the roof to evacuate the ambassador. And the later police counterattack was violent: four dead and nine hundred wounded.

The Nile was no longer a long, tranquil river.

Amerika-el-Latiniya Street, which led to the U.S. embassy, was completely blocked by a crowd of militant Islamists sitting on carpets in the street. Around them hung color posters calling for the release of Omar Abdel-Rahman, the old blind sheikh serving a life sentence in the United States for his role in the first World Trade Center attack in 1993. Other banners above the street showed the sheikh in a turban, with dark glasses and a full beard.

That the silent demonstration was permanent said a great deal about the Muslim Brotherhood's influence in Egypt.

Malko stepped around a couple of demonstrators and made his way to a barrier in front of the embassy manned by armed and wary Egyptian soldiers stationed behind chicanes and sandbags.

After a laborious conversation, it took a good ten minutes before an embassy employee appeared, a badge-wearing young woman whose shape suggested she'd been eating too many Turkish delights. She led Malko through the no-man's-land to the pink building that housed diplomatic services.

"Mr. Tombstone is expecting you," she said.

"Turkish, American, or espresso?"

Jerry Tombstone recited the choices in a slow, somewhat deliberate voice.

"Espresso, please," said Malko. This would be the first time he got a decent cup of coffee in an American embassy, he thought.

Tombstone went to a Nespresso machine in the back of his office. The Cairo CIA station chief was burly and very tall, and moved like a rugby player. But his bespoke striped shirt and red tie suggested a certain sophistication.

Malko studied Tombstone as he returned with the coffee. He had tufts of red hair on a balding scalp, a long nose, and a look of quiet intelligence, slow but sharp. He looked more like a Harvard professor than a CIA operative.

"Your mission in this beautiful country should give you a rest after your recent adventures," he said as Malko savored his espresso. "I hope you like the sun! My skin can't take it, so I go out as little as possible. Besides, there's nothing to do in this damn city."

He paused.

"You know why you're in Cairo, don't you?"

"No. You'll have to tell me."

"So nobody talked. Excellent."

Tombstone gave a dry chuckle and handed Malko a packet of photos from his desk.

"Let's start with these," he said.

The pictures were all of the same person, a gorgeous woman with long blond hair. She appeared in a variety of settings. First, getting out of a red Austin Mini with a British license plate, showing off a pair of very long legs. Then, wearing different outfits: an evening dress, an almost severe pants suit, a miniskirt, boots. The last shots had been taken during a bathing suit fashion show and displayed almost all of the unknown woman's magnificent body. On one photo Malko noticed an amused look in her almond-shaped eyes and a greedy pout.

Malko put the photos down and grinned.

"A married man's impossible dream!" he said. "I'm guessing she's not in London anymore; otherwise, that's where I'd be."

"You're right. She's staying at the same place you are. The Four Seasons, Room 2704."

"Is she expecting me?"

"Not really," said Tombstone with a slight smile, "but I'm counting on you to get to know her. I don't think that should be too hard."

"What makes you say so?"

"Cynthia Mulligan is a fairly well-known model in London. She lives in an elegant Chelsea studio and doesn't seem to have money problems. MI5 has been keeping an eye on her. They say she's bisexual, on a ratio of about one man to twenty women. We know some of her girlfriends, but not all of them."

"Given her profile, what makes you think she'll fall for me? You'd do better to send a woman."

Tombstone gave a short laugh.

"Our antidiscrimination rules don't let us do that! Anyway, Ted Boteler in special ops claims you're able to seduce any woman alive."

The CIA station chief's tone was light, but Malko knew he wasn't joking.

"I'm prepared to use my charm in a good cause," he said. "So what is this ravishing creature doing in Cairo?"

"She's here with her boyfriend. This man, here."

Tombstone brought a new packet of photos from his desk. These were a lot less glamorous. They showed a very well-dressed dark-skinned man with short, curly hair and a face like Barack Obama's.

"This is Mulligan's current lover, Prince Ibrahim al-Senussi, a Libyan businessman. He's rich, lives in Belgravia in London, and is madly in love with her."

Malko looked up sharply.

"That isn't going to make things easy."

Tombstone airily dismissed the Libyan prince with a wave of his freckled hand.

"I doubt that many of your conquests were just lying around waiting for you to show up," he said. "Anyway, this is no game. You have to deliver."

Any apparent lightness had disappeared.

"I suspect my seduction enterprise isn't the entire mission," said Malko.

"That's right. It's just the easiest and most pleasant part. We absolutely need to learn some things, and it's only by getting close to Cynthia Mulligan that we have a chance of finding them out."

"Women don't always talk," objected Malko. "They protect the men they love."

"I doubt Mulligan is in love with al-Senussi," said Tombstone dryly.

"But she's here with him in Cairo, and I imagine they sleep in the same bed."

The American gave an ironic smile.

"He's crazy about her, and let's say she puts up with it."

"So why is she in Cairo, if she doesn't have feelings for him?"

Tombstone sighed and ran a hand over his bald scalp.

"I don't know that much about women," he admitted, "but they often act on complicated motives. From what we've determined, al-Senussi went to great lengths to get her to take the trip. He's very rich. Maybe Mulligan felt like seeing the Pyramids or spending a pleasant vacation in a palace."

"Let's suppose you're right and I'm able to seduce her. What is the name of the game?"

Leaning back in his armchair, Jerry Tombstone spoke slowly and distinctly:

"We want to find out who tried to kill them eight days ago, in a particularly brutal way, along with two hundred and seventy-seven other people."

CHAPTER 3

"Not exactly a targeted killing," said Malko with a touch of black humor.

"If the attack had succeeded, every passenger on Flight 132 would be dead," Tombstone said.

"So what happened, exactly?"

"BA 132 from London was on final approach, coming in at very low altitude. As it flew over the airport perimeter, one of the pilots saw a man on top of a van pointing what looked like a portable surface-to-air missile at the plane."

"What then?"

"The pilot was scared out of his wits, of course. But he saw the missile fly harmlessly under the plane just before the 777's wheels touched down."

"Did they find the shooter?"

"No. From what we've been able to figure out, he fired a SAM-14 Strela. It's a heat-seeking missile and should have flown into one of the jet's engines and blown everything up. But two miracles happened.

"First, the infrared guidance system didn't work, so it missed its target. Otherwise, bye-bye, Boeing. Second, the missile's autodestruct mechanism, which should have blown it up fourteen to eighteen seconds after missing the target, didn't work either. Mukhabarat agents found the Strela on the runway the following morning, intact. Our Egyptian colleagues gave us its serial numbers right away, of course. They know that our database is much more complete than theirs.

"We found that the Strela was part of a batch of five hundred missiles delivered to Libya in 1998 by Rosoboronexport, the Russian state arms sales agency. We even learned that the Libyans asked the Russians for much more modern SAMs but were turned down. They gave them a batch of Strelas that weren't being manufactured anymore instead. Our missile probably didn't work because it hadn't been maintained. The Russians feel that Strelas aren't worth a damn after ten years."

Puzzled, Malko asked, "How could a SAM delivered to Qaddafi in Libya thirteen years ago turn up here in Cairo?"

"We have a theory," said the CIA station chief. "It involves a very dangerous Islamist named Abu Bukatalla. If you don't mind a short lecture, I'll tell you all about him."

Malko sat back in his armchair, and Tombstone continued.

"From documents recovered in Tripoli, we know these Strelas were stored in a Libyan army barracks in Bayda, a city east of Benghazi," he said. "Two days after the February 17 Revolution, a mob of insurgents drove Qaddafi's soldiers out and ransacked the depot, down to the last cartridge."

"What became of the weapons?" asked Malko.

"Well, we've found one of them, at least," the American said with an ironic smile. "The others just vanished. A lot were looted by the Libyans; others were probably shipped south to Niger and Mali, to reinforce the militias of al-Qaeda in the Islamic Maghreb. French intelligence alerted us that AQIM members came to Benghazi shopping for weapons. Some of the matériel went to Egypt. In fact, the Egyptian army intercepted two trucks crammed with weapons: AK-47s, RPG-7s, and ammunition. We aren't really concerned about that. But this is the first sign of the stock of forty Strelas stored at Bayda."

"Weren't they sent to Gaza?"

"That's a distinct possibility," said Tombstone, "but not necessarily to Hamas. Probably a radical Salafist group there called the Jund Ansar Allah that is financed by Qatar, Saudi Arabia, and Yemen. And this is important: they're also linked with the Egyptian Muslim Brotherhood's clandestine branch, which in turn is close to Abu Bukatalla, the head of a Libyan *takfiri* militia. *Takfiri* are the most extreme Islamists. They consider Muslims who don't agree with them to be apostates who deserve to have their throats cut."

"So what does Abu Bukatalla have to do with al-Senussi?" asked Malko.

"From wiretaps, we know Abu Bukatalla is intimately connected to Qatar and wants to build an Islamic caliphate in Libya," said the CIA station chief. "The last thing Abu Bukatalla wants is a modern monarch backed by the West."

As Malko listened to Tombstone's presentation, he became more and more perplexed.

"Are you saying that Abu Bukatalla wanted to kill al-Senussi so badly that he would sacrifice all the other passengers on the flight?" he asked. "There are easier ways of getting rid of people."

"It wouldn't be the first time," said Tombstone.

"In 1989, the Libyan secret services put a bomb in a rigged suitcase aboard a UTA flight from Libreville to N'Djamena and Paris. It blew up over the Ténéré region, killing everyone on board. The Libyans had heard that a notorious opponent of Colonel Qaddafi would be on the flight. Luckily for him, he missed the plane. But the other passengers died. For nothing."

A hush descended on the CIA station chief's office. It was wearing a black armband.

"But it must be easy to kill somebody in a city like Cairo," said Malko.

"That's right, but the targeted assassination of a Libyan in Cairo would have embarrassed the Muslim Brotherhood. They're running in the parliamentary elections in a few weeks and are keeping a low profile."

"Shooting down a passenger plane isn't exactly low profile," Malko pointed out.

"It could be blamed on the Gaza extremists. They've already attacked Israelis in Eilat from Egyptian soil," said Tombstone.

"But that still leaves a big question: why kill Ibrahim al-Senussi?"

The CIA station chief looked as pleased as a teacher who was finally being asked an intelligent question.

"That's *the* big question," he said. "I assume my colleague in Vienna didn't mention Operation Sunrise to you, did he?"

"No, he didn't," said Malko, once again reminded of the American mania for giving poetic names to their operations.

"Well then, let me fill you in."

As he warmed to his subject, Tombstone sounded even more like a professor than a CIA operative.

"First we have to back up a little," he said. "In 2003, when Colonel Qaddafi yielded to our friendly persuasion and quit trying to get nuclear weapons, we became friends again. He was still a nut job, of course, but he was *our* nut job. The friendly persuasion consisted of threatening to bomb Libya back to the Stone Age if he kept trying to go nuclear.

"Besides, we had a common enemy: the Islamists and al-Qaeda. Qaddafi started helping us—a lot. And we helped him too, pointing out people who might hurt him and giving him surveillance equipment. Everything was going along swimmingly until the revolt erupted in Benghazi in February 2011. At first, we weren't too worried. Qaddafi's army could easily wipe out the demonstrators, who were untrained and poorly armed. But then France went to the barricades in the name of human rights and dragged Great Britain and the others into the anti-Qaddafi crusade. Pretty soon, their jets were flying over Libya.

"Well, you know the rest: Qaddafi could defeat his opponents, but he couldn't take on NATO. And we soon realized that among Qaddafi's opponents, the only organized ones were the Islamists. The rest were what Lenin would call 'useful idiots.'

"So the Agency got to work and soon discovered a disturbing secret: the role of Qatar. Officially, Qatar had sided with the rebels, giving them money and weapons. But we discovered that the emir Sheikh Hamad had secretly decided to take over the Libyan revolution."

"Qatar's a long way from Libya," Malko objected. "And Qatar has its own oil, so it doesn't need any."

"That's right, but there's a link between the two countries: the Salabi family, who are dyed-in-the-wool Islamists opposed to Qaddafi. Three brothers.

"Qaddafi threw Ali Salabi in prison in the 1980s. When he got out, he was exiled and took refuge in Qatar. There he was welcomed with open arms by a Brotherhood theologian, Yusuf al-Qaradawi, who preaches on Al Jazeera that it's apostasy for a Muslim to support a secular constitution in Libya."

"Very reassuring," remarked Malko.

"You said it! Ali Salabi persuaded the emir of Qatar to support the anti-Qaddafi rebels, starting with his brother Ismail Salabi, who founded the February 17 Brigade with the help of money and weapons from Qatar.

"After that, all of Libya's radical Islamists got on board. Abdelhakim Belhadj, who'd been a jihadist in Afghanistan and close to Osama bin Laden; Abdelhakim al-Hasadi, trained by the Taliban; Abu Sufian bin Qumu, a jihadist released from Guantanamo in 2007; and finally our *takfiri* friend Abu Bukatalla."

"None of this sounds very encouraging," said Malko.

"That's why the Agency decided to step in. We wanted to create a party that wasn't Islamist or anti-Western. The trouble is, the Libyans who like us aren't a military force. So we thought of looking at the leadership.

"Mustafa Abdel-Jalil, the current head of the National Transitional Council, isn't exactly kosher. He was Qaddafi's justice minister and twice called for the death penalty against the Bulgarian nurses that Qaddafi accused of giving Libyan children AIDS back in 1998. If he became the head of a new Libya, people would be up in arms.

"So our British cousins put forth the name Ibrahim al-Senussi.

He has some real pluses: he's the grandson of King Idris, whom Qaddafi overthrew, the rebels have adopted his grandfather's flag, and he's pro-Western. In short, al-Senussi is Operation Sunrise."

"He sounds ideal," said Malko.

Tombstone grimaced.

"Not quite. In the beginning, al-Senussi didn't want to do it. His MI6 handler had to really twist his arm to convince him. And he couldn't tell him that the CIA was behind the operation, because it would scare him off. Al-Senussi isn't crazy, and he first wanted to see if he had support in Libya before making his decision. That's why he came to Cairo."

"So where does Cynthia Mulligan fit in this picture?"

"Nowhere. She's just R and R."

"But this doesn't tell me who tried to kill him," insisted Malko. "Don't you think the National Transitional Council would take umbrage at al-Senussi's ambitions? Many countries recognize the council as the new Libya. Officially, the NTC governs the country."

The American gave him a patient look.

"The NTC pretends to govern, but it doesn't have any real power in the interior. Several of its members have already quit. Besides, the Libyan resistance is extremely divided. It's made up of about forty militias who all distrust each other."

"But they managed to take over the country."

"Yeah, thanks to NATO. And I'm sure you've noticed that post-Qaddafi Libya is now a free-form cluster fuck.

"Look at what happened in Tripoli. The city is taken from Qaddafi's people by militias from all over, helped by local rebels. So our friend Abdelhakim Belhadj proclaims himself governor of the city—a fact the NTC learns by watching the news on Al Jazeera. When they ask Belhadj to step aside for a civilian from the council, he tells them to get lost. I told you who Belhadj is, didn't I?"

"Pretty much, yes."

"Reading his résumé, even Amnesty International would gag," said Tombstone. "He was the Emir of Gick before heading to Afghanistan, where he meets and pledges fealty to Osama bin Laden. Later, he's arrested in Malaysia; the Agency interrogates him in Thailand, then turns him over to the Libyans, who put him in jail for six years. Can you guess who got him out?"

"No idea," said Malko.

"The current president of the NTC, Mustafa Abdel-Jalil. At the time, he was Qaddafi's minister of justice, and very religious. He considered Belhadj a good Muslim, so he persuaded the Guide to free him. You see how he's paying him back."

"So the NTC could have tried to eliminate al-Senussi."

"No, they don't have the means. But if we don't find out who tried to kill our candidate, we could have an anti-Western Islamic caliphate in Libya very soon. It would be an ideal hub for AQIM, Hamas, Tunisia, and of course Egypt's Muslim Brotherhood.

"The Arab Spring would turn into a Salafist winter. Libya's already an Islamist country under low-grade sharia law. True, they don't cut off a thief's hand, just a finger. But women are completely locked away, alcohol's forbidden, only religious marriage is allowed, people pray five times a day, and everybody's happy."

Seemingly exhausted by his apocalyptic vision, Tombstone poured himself a glass of water.

"You still haven't told me whom you suspect of trying to kill Ibrahim al-Senussi," said Malko.

"Well, we have a hunch, but no real proof."

"Why do you say 'we'?"

"I told you that Operation Sunrise had been initiated by the Cousins, right? Naturally they put a wiretap on al-Senussi. He was very reluctant to come to Cairo, would have preferred to do his pulse taking from London, up until the moment he was contacted by a Libyan emissary, one Shokri Mazen. Mazen suggested that Ibrahim meet Abu Bukatalla's representatives in Cairo, claiming that Abu Bukatalla was prepared to support him as a constitutional monarch."

"Wait—is this the same Bukatalla you were talking about earlier?"

"That's right: a *takfiri* at the head of a hard-core Islamist militia."

"That seems a very odd person to be supporting a future king."

"This Mazen claimed the Islamists had always had a good relationship with the Senussi tribe."

"And al-Senussi took his advice?"

"Yep, and promptly booked a flight to Cairo with the beautiful Cynthia Mulligan. But in the meantime the Cousins discovered that Mazen was spending all his time in the Qatari embassy in London, even though al-Senussi's project ran completely counter to Qatar's plans."

"So Mazen was playing a double game," concluded Malko, "luring al-Senussi to Cairo to shoot his plane down."

"Officially, we can't even speak of this. But very few people knew which flight our candidate for the throne was taking. Shokri Mazen was one of them."

Frankly shocked, Malko asked, "Are you telling me that Ibrahim al-Senussi was drawn here so he could be killed along with the passengers of BA Flight 132—on orders from Qatar?"

"You might very well think that," said Tombstone with a small smile. "I couldn't possibly comment."

"From what you've said, this Abu Bukatalla has connections with fundamentalist Islamists in Cairo," continued Malko. "He could have given them a surface-to-air missile."

"Anything's possible," said the American vaguely.

"I understand that the Agency is on good terms with the Mukhabarat. Why not ask them for a hand?"

"We already have. The Mukhabarat is very well informed, but they don't want to go after the Islamists two months before the elections. Still, I'm on excellent terms with General Mowafi, who replaced Omar Suleiman as head of the service because of his closeness to Mubarak.

"He put Nasser Ihab at your disposal, the agent who picked you up at the airport. It's for your safety but it's also to watch what we're doing. You can be sure that Nasser files a report every evening at Mukhabarat headquarters."

In Malko's mind, the pieces were starting to fall into place. But a big one remained.

"Why not ask al-Senussi himself? He might suspect who's after him."

Tombstone scowled. "That wouldn't be very smart. Al-Senussi doesn't know that someone tried to kill him. Nothing leaked to the press, and the passengers on the plane didn't notice anything. If we tell him, he might take the first flight for London with his sweetie. That would be the end of the game, and we don't have anybody to replace him."

"I understand your plan better now," said Malko. "But what's the point of seducing Cynthia Mulligan? You said yourself that she doesn't know what's going on."

"She's living with al-Senussi, so she'd be aware of his appointments, the people he sees, his telephone calls. If we learn that, we might be able to figure out who our prime suspects are."

"But even assuming she falls into my arms," asked Malko, "why should she tell me anything?"

CHAPTER 4

Despite its sweeping view of the Nile, the third-floor bar was deserted. A waiter rushed over and ushered the two men to a table overlooking Nasser Avenue and the river. Like most of the hotels in Cairo, the Four Seasons was three-quarters empty. The Arab Spring had decimated the tourist industry, reducing some of the guides who led camel rides around the Pyramids to eating their breadwinners to survive.

"Two mojitos," ordered Tombstone.

The mood in the room was closer to that of a wake than that of a trendy bar. Just as the mojitos arrived, three Gulf Arabs walked in, looking as gray as undertakers.

Malko turned to Tombstone.

"You sure they're going to come?"

The American gave a resigned smile.

"If not, at least we'll have had an excellent mojito."

"By the way, does Nasser know what I'm doing in Cairo?"

"No, of course not. I told the Mukhabarat you were here to check on Islamist groups that were getting out of hand."

Tombstone was sucking on his mojito straw when Malko saw his eyes go to the bar's entrance. He turned around to look and got what felt like a punch to the solar plexus. A couple was walking into the bar, and the atmosphere seemed to have suddenly warmed up. In stiletto heels, the woman walked like a runway model, her chest held very straight, head high, hair flowing down her shoulders. The bartender's eyes were popping out of his head, though the unknown woman's clothes were perfectly proper. A gray silk dress that ended above the knee, it didn't show any cleavage but it fit her like a glove.

When she passed their table, Malko could see that in spite of the modesty of her outfit, the silk clearly outlined her nipples.

The man walking behind the woman almost went unnoticed. Wearing a white shirt and black pants, he had curly hair, very dark skin, and coarse features.

The pair sat down at a nearby table, with the woman facing Tombstone and Malko. With natural ease, she crossed her legs high enough to display some thigh.

It was enough to give a man sweaty palms.

When their waiter came over, he kept his eyes fixed on the Nile, probably to maintain his professional cool.

When they had ordered—mojitos, also—al-Senussi took his companion's hand and held on to it.

He was probably afraid someone would steal her.

They didn't talk much. The young woman seemed intrigued by the riverboats that cruised up and down the Nile in a splash of neon lights and blaring Arab music. Malko had trouble taking his eyes off her. His "target" was a very beautiful woman, with eyes that gave her a feline look.

Tombstone leaned toward him over the table.

"Okay, let me take you to dinner. No point in hanging around here; it might attract attention. Our customer's in love, but that doesn't mean he's a fool. The main thing is, you've seen her."

Malko didn't argue. After all, he could hardly jump the young woman in the Libyan's presence.

Downstairs, they found Nasser chatting at the front desk. When he saw them, he promptly went to get behind the wheel of the Mercedes. As they took off, he said a few words in Arabic to Tombstone, who relayed the message.

"I asked him to find out about the couple in Room 2704. The guy at the desk said that al-Senussi ordered a limousine for seven o'clock tomorrow morning. He's going to Marsa Matruh."

"Where's that?"

"On the coast, beyond El Alamein. It's an ordinary seaside resort, about three hundred miles from Cairo."

"Is he checking out of the hotel?"

"No, just going for the day."

"With Cynthia Mulligan?"

"I suspect he has a meeting that involves his project, so he won't take her along. That gives you a free day to work on her."

They drove toward Tahrir Square—now empty of demonstrators—and turned into Qasr el-Nil. A few minutes later, in a busy street across from Saudi Airlines, the Mercedes pulled up at a wooden door inlaid with mother of pearl. A sign in Arabic and English read "The Arabesque."

"We're eating here," said Tombstone.

The place looked like a bar, with a big flat-screen television on the wall and deafening modern music. They walked around the counter into a small room on the right. Not many customers. A few men were chatting around a high, round table under the TV.

"The food isn't too bad," said the American. "*Mezzes* and fish. It's one of the fashionable places. Want a beer?"

"Is there anything else?" Though Austrian, Malko wasn't too big on beer.

"No."

"Okay, I'll have a beer, then."

Abu Bukatalla watched tensely as the road stretched ahead into the darkness. With his striped polo shirt, green khakis, and full beard, there was nothing especially distinctive about him. But the *takfiri* Bukatalla was one of the most dangerous men in Libya and the leader of a militia of about a hundred fanatics. He hated Qaddafi but refused to go to the front lines, unwilling to fight alongside NATO infidels.

A few miles before Sallum, a small Egypt-Libya border crossing, his driver left the paved Tobruk highway to take a dirt road running south of it that was used only by locals. They were less than a mile from the border, and night had fallen. In the front seat of the old Opel, Bukatalla's bodyguard held his folding AK-47 across his knees, safety off and a cartridge in the chamber. As one of the most radical Islamist leaders in Libya, Bukatalla had his enemies.

He took out his cell phone, dialed a Libyan number, and got an immediate answer. The conversation was very short. Feeling satisfied, he hung up.

Five minutes later, a pair of headlights flashed, briefly lighting up the road. The driver pulled over and Bukatalla climbed out of the Opel, followed by his bodyguard. They walked to a car parked nearby.

Its driver got out and hugged him.

"*Allahu akbar*, the man at the checkpoint is a friend," the man whispered.

The two Libyans climbed into the back of a very old Mercedes. It had Egyptian license plates, to avoid traffic stops. A car with Libyan plates could cross the border if it was driven by its owner, but you needed special insurance and had to register with the sometimes inquisitive immigration service.

They rode in silence for a few minutes, until the border crossing's lights appeared. Unlike the big checkpoint on the main highway, this one was tiny and used only by locals, mainly Egyptians who crossed into Libya to buy gasoline or dates. The driver stopped in front of a barrier painted with the Egyptian tricolor and guarded by a policeman. He rolled down his window and said a few words.

The policeman smiled and, without checking the interior of the car or opening the trunk, ordered a soldier to raise the barrier. He was a member of the Egyptian Muslim Brotherhood, which was working to establish an Islamic caliphate in Libya. He didn't know who the car's passengers were, only that its driver belonged to the same cell in Sallum that he did and that Cairo had given orders to let the car through.

The Mercedes quickly crossed the hamlet of Bir Jubnai, driving on a dirt road that ran parallel to the Sallum–Marsa Matruh highway. In about ten miles, after going over a pass, the driver angled north toward the highway. The Egyptian Army knew about the side road, of course, and occasionally set up checkpoints to catch arms smugglers. The soldiers wouldn't necessarily be members of the Muslim Brotherhood, either. So there was some risk.

Thirty miles of bumpy dirt road and an hour and a half

later, they reached the little coastal town of Sidi Barrani and the main highway, now free of checkpoints. It took them two more hours to reach Marsa Matruh.

Bukatalla was feeling on edge. He didn't like being in Egypt, at the mercy of the ferocious Mukhabarat. True, the Egyptians had switched sides, supporting the new rulers of Libya. In the beginning they even allowed Qatari planes to land at the Egyptian military airport in Sallum, where weapons were carried across the border to the rebels. Forgotten were the compromises of the Mubarak regime, which would occasionally accept suitcases full of cash in exchange for anti-Qaddafi opponents who had taken refuge in Egypt.

But the Mukhabarat was known for its shifting alliances and was close to the Americans.

Only an important reason would have led Bukatalla to cross into Egypt. But his initial plan to kill al-Senussi had failed, and he now had to come up with a Plan B, one that might have other advantages.

The driver stopped the Mercedes in front of a square house far from downtown and honked. A young man immediately opened the wooden door, and Bukatalla entered a room with old carpets on the ground and food set out in bowls.

A lanky man in a white robe jumped up and hugged him. He was very thin, with a gaunt face, prominent nose, and fierce eyes. He sat down with Bukatalla near the *mezzes* and bowls of lamb and rice.

Bukatalla glared him.

"Why did Allah not guide your arm properly, brother?" the *takfiri* asked reproachfully. "Have you committed sins that angered him?"

Abdul Gamal al-Afghani bowed his head, muttering that his soul was as pure as crystal. It wasn't his fault that the damned Strela made by infidels hadn't worked.

He had done everything properly, he said. Naturally, he was surprised not to hear the Boeing 777 explode, and now it was too late for another attempt. Still, he was prepared to try again if Bukatalla wanted him to.

The militia leader listened thoughtfully. This wasn't the first time that a ground-to-air missile had misfired. And he had complete confidence in al-Afghani, who was a member of the Muslim Brotherhood and had fought the Americans in Afghanistan. He had come back to Egypt and become the *takfiri*'s liaison with their friends in Gaza.

Bukatalla had ordered thirty Strelas stolen from al-Qaeda to be delivered to al-Afghani as a way to strengthen the extremist Gaza group. So when Bukatalla's emissary asked him to fire one of them at a British Airways jet—without telling him why, of course—he couldn't very well refuse.

The trouble was, the failure of the attack was forcing Abu Bukatalla to change all his plans. Normally the al-Senussi problem would have been settled by now. The order to eliminate him had come from Qatar, and Bukatalla had obeyed without argument. Now he had to devise an alternative strategy to eliminate the man in the pay of the infidels.

The only thing the *takfiri* could think of was to draw him into Libya, where he would be easier to kill. Al-Senussi himself had given him the idea when he asked for a meeting—though in Egypt, not Libya—because Bukatalla was one of the Islamist leaders whose support he hoped to win.

So Bukatalla decided on a two-stage plan. First, lure al-Senussi into Libya to meet possible supporters. Bukatalla didn't know who they might be, so this would allow him to unmask and kill them. That done, he would kill al-Senussi himself.

In the end, it would be even more effective than the plan hatched in Qatar.

Bukatalla was taking a risk by agreeing to travel to Marsa Matruh to meet al-Senussi, who might have the Mukhabarat on his tail. But that was a risk he decided to take. Establishing an Islamic caliphate in Libya was worth taking some chances.

Feeling more cheerful, he dipped a piece of pita bread in a bowl of hummus. He was hungry.

Al-Afghani was watching him anxiously, and Bukatalla gave the man a reassuring smile.

"I believe you, brother. You haven't committed any sins."

Reassured, the Egyptian began to eat some lentil soup. He felt annoyed at having missed the British Airways plane. In Afghanistan he had hit much more difficult targets. He prayed to Allah for a chance to redeem himself.

The television set was still blaring when the plate of *mezzes* finally arrived: hummus, falafel, meatballs, lamb sausages, and stuffed peppers. The Arabesque was full now, mainly with men sitting at the bar and drinking beer under a row of unusual chandeliers made of empty bottles.

Malko watched as Tombstone fed his big carcass, tearing through the *mezzes* like a lion devouring a gazelle. Suddenly Malko noticed a couple heading their way.

"Jerry!" he muttered. "Take a look."

The American grabbed a last meatball and looked up to see al-Senussi and his shapely companion take a table near theirs.

When the young woman looked around, her gaze fell on Malko and Tombstone. She gave Malko a surprised and amused glance, then turned her attention to the menu.

"God's on our side," said Tombstone. "They can't suspect us of following them."

"So what? We've already seen them."

"Yes, but she noticed you. When you talk to her back at the hotel, she'll remember you."

The two men finished their dinner. The desserts on the menu looked pretty terrible, so they ordered only coffee.

The CIA station chief's cell phone chimed, and he answered it.

"Hm, they've attacked the Israeli embassy again. I imagine we'll be next on the list. The Egyptians are sick of the old Mubarak pro-Israel politics. This is all gonna end badly."

When they stood up, al-Senussi's companion turned her head slightly, this time looking directly at Malko. He looked back. Their eyes locked for a few seconds; then she looked down and went back to cutting a very old lamb chop.

Outside, the heat was heavy. A few volleys of automatic gunfire clattered in the distance.

"I have to go back to the embassy to send a telegram," said Tombstone with a sigh. "Anyway, this is a night to celebrate."

"Why?"

"Because you've made eye contact. When that beautiful blonde looked at you, it wasn't casual. Now you just have to try your luck."

"Let's hope our friend Ibrahim doesn't take his sweetheart to the seaside."

"Tomorrow should be your day."

CHAPTER 5

Sitting at the wheel of the Mercedes, Nasser watched the entrance of the Four Seasons. The previous evening, Jerry Tombstone had asked him to check if al-Senussi was actually going to Marsa Matruh. He was now inconspicuously parked among the taxis and tourist vans. He yawned. It was ten past seven in the morning, and al-Senussi should have left the hotel at seven. A few moments later, Nasser abruptly straightened in his seat: the Libyan had just appeared, alone.

Al-Senussi got into a big white Cherokee that immediately headed north on the Corniche el-Nil, with Nasser close behind. As usual, traffic was terrible. The cars worked their way through a maze of streets leading to the Ring Road, which would eventually lead them to the highway to El Alamein. That was one of the country's main arteries, and driving would be easier despite the heavy truck traffic. There were gas stations and truck stops everywhere, with semis lined up in the rest areas.

At Abar el-Brins the highway led to Alexandria, and the Cherokee took the road along the coast to El Alamein. Nasser stayed a good distance behind. It looked as if al-Senussi was indeed heading to Marsa Matruh, a hundred miles ahead.

Suddenly Nasser saw the same green Toyota in his rear-view mirror that he had first noticed when they were leaving Cairo. He cautiously pulled off near a café to let it pass. There was no danger of losing his target: there was only one highway. Nasser waited for a few minutes, then drove on. He easily caught up with the Toyota, which was staying close behind the Cherokee.

So al-Senussi was being followed, but by whom? Nasser was there, so it wasn't the Mukhabarat. Keeping a safe distance back, he jotted down the Toyota's license number. A lone young man, bearded, was driving. The beard alone didn't mean much in Egypt these days; Nasser had one, too.

It took them an hour to get to Marsa Matruh. I'll be putting in nearly eight hundred miles today, Nasser thought ruefully. For a joke of a salary.

Hunger woke Malko. The food at the Arabesque didn't stick to the ribs. After a quick shower he went down to the breakfast room.

It was nearly empty, aside from a white woman helping herself at the buffet: Cynthia Mulligan, piling croissants and toast on her plate. She was wearing tight shorts and an equally tight tank top. Malko took a plate and walked over to the buffet, arranging to wind up facing her.

They almost bumped into each other. Cynthia looked up and blinked. With a smile, Malko asked:

"Didn't you have dinner at the Arabesque last night?"

"That's right."

"So did I. I was there with my boss. You were the most beautiful woman in the room."

Cynthia smiled in turn.

"That's not saying much. There were only men there."

They were facing each other, plates in hand. Malko took the initiative.

"Are you by yourself?"

"Yes."

"Care to join me?"

"No, let's sit at my table. My things are there."

When they were seated, he introduced himself.

"My name's Malko Linge. I'm Austrian, and I'm in the oil business. I'm waiting to get into Libya to start the refineries running again. In the meantime, I'm hanging out in Cairo, but there's not much to do here. What about you? What are you doing in Egypt?"

Cynthia took a bite of croissant and said:

"I'm on vacation with my boyfriend. He went to Marsa Matruh for the day."

"What does he do?"

"He's a businessman. He's Libyan, and he's in import-export."

"Will you be staying in Cairo long?"

"I don't know."

They ate their breakfast, chatting about this and that. Malko watched the young woman, who occasionally shot him curious looks. He clearly intrigued her.

When they were finished, she glanced at her watch.

"I have to go now. I'm off to visit the Pyramids. You can't go too late; otherwise, it's too hot."

"When will you be back?"

"Around two or three. Then I'll go up to the pool on the fifth floor."

She stood up and added, "Maybe I'll see you later."

She clearly wasn't avoiding him. But Malko didn't offer to accompany her. That would have been a bit much.

He'd simply have to wait.

He did a quick calculation. Given the distance, al-Senussi probably wouldn't get back until late that night. That gave him a chance.

The El-Aluina Hotel deck overlooked an empty blue sea. Marsa Matruh didn't have many visitors at this time of year.

Stirring his cup of coffee, al-Senussi yawned. He had decided to make the tiring trip here after being contacted by a man called Nabil, who'd been sent by his London contact, Shokri Mazen. Nabil would introduce him to Abu Bukatalla, the man who originally persuaded him to fly to Cairo and seemed prepared to support his candidacy.

At ten past ten, a young bearded man came up to al-Senussi's table.

"The person you want to see is waiting for you," he announced with a smile.

"Where is he?"

"Not far from here."

When al-Senussi hesitated, the young man added:

"We have to be careful. The person you want to see is not here officially."

Satisfied, al-Senussi followed him to a small white Honda in the parking lot. Two men were standing nearby, watching their surroundings. A ten-minute trip took them to an isolated square house on the southern outskirts, its shutters closed. Al-Senussi could just make out a man inside, seated on a carpet set with plates of food and bottles of soda and mineral water.

The man stood up briskly and walked toward him, arms outstretched.

"*Allahu akbar!*" he cried in a pleasant baritone. "You're here at last!"

He gave al-Senussi a lengthy embrace, then stepped back, smiling brightly. With his round face, black beard, and striped brown shirt, Bukatalla looked reassuring. Only his brown kaffiyeh, one corner hanging over his right shoulder, suggested anything Islamic.

Impressed by the warm welcome, al-Senussi forgot the four-hundred-odd miles he had just driven. Following his host's example, he sat down on the carpet set with *mezzes* and bottles of soda, and the two men began to eat.

When they'd eaten their fill, Bukatalla took a swig of soda and broke the silence:

"I'm sure I'm not the only person you want to meet in Libya to outline your project," he said. "But I'm prepared to help, and I might be useful. What are your plans?"

Bukatalla's welcome had put al-Senussi in a confiding mood, and he didn't hesitate to talk. He was walking on air. Conquering Libya was turning out to be easier than expected.

"I have to meet with General Abdul Fatah Younes," he said. "I spoke with a member of his tribe in London who gave me the phone number of his favorite nephew, Abd al-Raziq. I want to ask him to come to Cairo but haven't been able to reach him."

Like many Islamists, Abu Bukatalla had a special hatred for Younes, who had been Qaddafi's defense minister and had hunted them for the forty-two years of Qaddafi's rule. But his face betrayed nothing.

"That's an excellent idea, brother," he said approvingly. "General Younes is an important person, and his Obeidi tribe is powerful. But it's almost impossible to reach him from Cairo. First, because the phones don't work, and second, because General Younes is operating west of Benghazi, out of Brega or Ra's Lanuf. I'm sure he would be glad to meet you in Benghazi, but he definitely won't come to Cairo. He's too well known."

Al-Senussi felt himself coming down to earth. MI6 had warned him against traveling to Libya for the time being, because some NTC members took a dim view of his ambition to rise to power.

"Going to Benghazi would be dangerous," he objected.

"Not if you're under my protection," said Bukatalla, hand on heart. "You can cross the border discreetly and stay at a safe house. From there you can easily contact General Younes's nephew. By the Prophet, I guarantee your security. No one will know you are in the country."

"There are Egyptians who are in contact with the NTC. They mustn't know I'm in Libya."

"They will know nothing," said Bukatalla. "We'll cross the border secretly, as I did to come here."

Just then, the muezzin at a nearby mosque began chanting, calling the faithful to prayer. It was half past twelve.

"Let's pray," suggested Bukatalla. "You can draw inspiration from what Allah the all-powerful and all-merciful tells you."

He unrolled a prayer rug and stood up. Al-Senussi didn't have one and had to make do with part of the carpet they'd been eating on.

He turned to face Mecca and knelt. Having always lived in the West, al-Senussi felt no particular sympathy for Islamists, but he knew he couldn't do without them if he wanted to gain any kind of power in Libya. And Bukatalla's welcome warmed his heart.

Sitting on the El-Aluina Hotel terrace, Nasser struggled to contain his impatience. His first impulse had been to follow al-Senussi when they came to pick him up. Nasser followed them to the parking lot, where he immediately spotted two men guarding the Honda that al-Senussi got into. They stayed behind when the car took off, clearly making sure it wasn't followed.

There was nothing to be done. The main thing was not to alert his adversaries. But the upshot was that Nasser didn't know whom al-Senussi was meeting.

Prayer was over, and the two men were sitting on the carpet again. Bukatalla broke the silence:

"Did Allah inspire you, brother?"

"I've decided to take your advice," said al-Senussi. "But everything has to be completely secret."

Bukatalla remained impassive.

"It's the will of Allah," he said in a tone that suggested he had a direct line to God. "I'm going to arrange your trip, and when it's ready, I'll have our brothers in Cairo contact you. Brother Nabil, whom you met, will simply tell you to go to Marsa Matruh. I'll take care of everything."

"Will I be away for long?"

"Just a few days, inshallah, but the unexpected can always happen. Communications aren't easy, and Qaddafi's dogs are prowling everywhere. Just trust me."

"I do trust you."

Al-Senussi hadn't dared mention Cynthia. He could hardly imagine showing up to meet the Islamists with a creature they would see as so provocative. Well, that was just too bad; she could wait for him in Cairo.

He looked at his watch.

"I have to leave now. I still have a long trip back to Cairo."

"May Allah keep you in his holy protection," said Bukatalla. "You'll hear from me soon, inshallah."

Malko was watching an unusual couple that had just sat down near the Four Seasons' swimming pool. The fifth-floor pool was open to the sky but unfortunately faced away from the Nile and was surrounded by high walls.

The man had a well-trimmed beard and was wearing a tan djellaba and sandals. He was holding the hand of a woman dressed in black from head to toe, her face hidden by a *niqab* with just a slit for her eyes. A vertical strip of cloth over her nose connected the two parts of the *niqab*. It was a strange couple to encounter in this modern tourist hotel, but they seemed quite at ease.

Malko started at the sound of a woman's voice.

"Didn't you wait for me?"

He turned around. Cynthia Mulligan was standing behind him, her eyes hidden behind dark glasses. She was wearing a miniskirt that ended well above her knees, and high heels.

Drop-dead gorgeous.

Malko noticed the shimmer of stockings on her legs. That was unexpected, and a good sign. A well-behaved woman wore stockings only for funerals.

"I'd forgotten all about you," he pretended. "Would you like a drink?"

"With pleasure."

Her skirt slid up when she sat on the bench facing him, revealing most of her thighs.

Cynthia caught Malko's look and said with a laugh, "Are you wondering why I wear stockings in this heat? It's because of the mosquitoes. They're everywhere and they've been dive-bombing my legs."

"I wasn't thinking of mosquitoes. They look very good on you."

"Thank you. I often wear stockings in London, and not because of mosquitoes."

"How were the Pyramids?"

"Dusty. And it was beastly hot. I had the feeling that I'd already seen them, because they show up on TV and in newspapers so often. Also, I thought the guide was going to attack me. His eyes were popping out of his head. When he helped me onto a camel, I thought he'd never take his hand off my bum."

Malko laughed heartily. "See that woman with the bearded man over there? That's what men here are used to. Obviously when a creature like you shows up, it's heaven on earth."

"They're mad," Cynthia said with a sigh. "Can I have a mojito?"

Nasser was trailing al-Senussi's Cherokee from a safe distance. They had just passed El Alamein, and the green Toyota that had followed the Cherokee on the way to Marsa Matruh was still behind it. A protective cordon. Nasser hoped the Toyota hadn't noticed him. It could just be someone guarding al-Senussi, but Nasser knew it wasn't the Mukhabarat. He had to find out who and why. They would reach Cairo at nightfall, he figured, if traffic wasn't too bad. Jerry Tombstone and his superiors would be glad to learn more about al-Senussi's escapade in Marsa Matruh.

Cynthia was drinking a second mojito when her cell rang. The conversation was very short, and the young woman lit a cigarette. She seemed relaxed, so Malko ventured a suggestion:

"Would you like to have dinner somewhere?"

She smiled at him apologetically.

"Sorry, no. My boyfriend just rang; he's coming back this evening. Maybe some other time."

"I'd like that very much," said Malko, giving her a long look.

Cynthia smiled before standing up.

"So would I. We'll see."

She walked away and Malko's eyes followed her swaying gait. She really was beautiful, he thought. He would have taken an interest in her even without his CIA orders. The way she moved, smiled, and looked at him all suggested she was a free woman.

Before entering the hotel, she turned and gave him a little wave.

Karim Akhdar had barely glanced at Ibrahim al-Senussi's companion. Partly because she was an infidel, an impure creature who dressed like a whore, but mainly because that wasn't the reason he was there.

His target was the blond foreigner she was drinking with. Akhdar belonged to Al-Tanzim al-Asasi, the Muslim Brotherhood's clandestine branch. His superior had told him to observe the Libyan and his girlfriend to find out whom they met with, and he was doing his job. Akhdar's wife, who accompanied him, didn't know this—and never would.

Akhdar took a sip of soda and decided to find out more about the foreigner with the blond hair.

The man was signing his check, which meant he was staying at the hotel. Akhdar strolled over to the bar, reaching the cash register at the same time as the waiter. He casually took the check from the tray and glanced at it, noting two pieces of information: the unknown man's name and his room number, 2621.

The waiter looked at Akhdar with surprise but merely smiled. You didn't cross bearded men these days. The Muslim Brothers might be ruling Egypt in a few months' time, and they had long memories.

Feeling pleased, Akhdar went back to his table. All he had to do now was pass on his information. How it would be used wasn't his concern.

The guard manning the checkpoint at the entrance to the Sofitel yanked at his dog's leash. The old Labrador hauled itself upright, sniffed vaguely around the taxi, and went back to its nap.

Not much of a line of defense against a possible car bomb.

The soldier responsible for stopping terrorist attacks against the hotel paused for a few seconds, captivated by the long blond hair he could glimpse in the back of the taxi. Tourism had dried up in Cairo, and the few visitors still around were aged retirees who had come to die at the foot of the Pyramids.

The taxi took the ramp to the Sofitel tower entrance. Located at the northern point of Roda Island, the hotel was hideous by day and spangled with green neon lights by night, but it did have one attraction: you could eat at an outdoor terrace overlooking the Nile.

Al-Senussi waited until a porter opened the taxi door before taking his hand off Cynthia's thigh. When she stepped out of the car, the bell captain caught his breath. Her black dress was so short, it was practically a belt, and she had sheathed her legs in dark stockings again because of mosquitoes.

When she and al-Senussi were settled on the terrace near the river and he'd ordered Cynthia a mojito—he knew her tastes—he raised his glass.

"Here's to our vacation. Are you enjoying Egypt?"

The young woman pouted.

"It's kind of grubby, but at least it's warm. And the people are nice."

Al-Senussi wondered how to break the news that he would be leaving her alone in Cairo for a couple of days. As it turned out, she raised the subject herself.

"Did your meeting go well?" she asked.

She wasn't especially interested in his project, but she had good manners. Al-Senussi jumped at the opening.

"It went very, very well," he boasted. "In fact, I think I'll be traveling to Libya."

"That's great," said Cynthia. "It'll be a change from Cairo. I hear there are nice beaches there."

Al-Senussi ducked his head, seeking refuge in his mojito. He and Cynthia were clearly on different wavelengths.

"Libya's a pretty lousy place, you know," he said carefully. "The food's bad, and there's still fighting going on. And the hotels—"

Cynthia didn't give up so easily.

"That's great! I'll be able to send my girlfriends postcards. Everybody's talking about Libya these days."

"There's no mail service. Phones, either. It's very hard—"

"No problem, we'll tour the countryside."

"It's just desert; there's nothing to see. And it's still dangerous."

By now, al-Senussi's reluctance was starting to get to her.

"What's this all about?" she demanded. "Don't you want to take me with you? Do you have another woman there?"

Stung, the Libyan was forced to show his hand.

"Of course not!" he protested indignantly. "It's just that Libya is a very conservative country. I'm going to be meeting with religious people. You can't come with me. And besides, there are no pyramids there."

"I don't mind. It'll be fun."

When Cynthia looked up, she caught al-Senussi's look of alarm and realized he really did have a problem.

"Oh well," she said with a sigh. "No matter. When you take off for your crappy country, I'll fly back to London. There are lots of great parties right now. It's Fashion Week."

This stopped al-Senussi in his tracks. He had no illusions about Cynthia's true feelings for him and could already see her in the arms of some husky photographer.

He put his hand on hers.

"All right, I'll take you to Libya. I just hope you won't be disappointed."

Malko ate dinner in his room. Going down to the restaurant alone felt depressing, and he didn't want to be seen with Jerry Tombstone too much.

Besides, the image of Cynthia Mulligan was dancing in his head. Now he *really* wanted to seduce her. With her cat's eyes and statuesque body, she was wildly attractive.

Unfortunately, al-Senussi had returned from Marsa Matruh, which wasn't going to make things easy.

A tourist boat cruised down the Nile past the Sofitel dining terrace in a glare of neon light and the boom of Arab music being played for its three passengers.

"Let's go back to the hotel!" said Cynthia.

Al-Senussi was eager to capitalize on his promise, especially since Cynthia seemed more desirable than ever this evening.

There was just one hitch: how would Abu Bukatalla react when he showed up at Marsa Matruh with Cynthia? Even if she were bundled up from head to toe, any devout Muslim would see her as demonic. And Bukatalla was a lot more than devout. He'd have a woman like Cynthia stoned.

The moment they were in the elevator, al-Senussi couldn't resist grabbing the young woman's breasts. He pinched her nipples so hard that she complained.

"Hey, take it easy! You don't have to twist them like doorknobs."

"But you said your breasts were very sensitive."

"That's true," she snapped, "but not when you try and rip them off."

Annoyed, al-Senussi went for her dress instead and managed to tear off Cynthia's panties before they reached the twenty-seventh floor. His prick was so stiff, he could have cracked nuts with it.

Azuz Gait drove his little red motorbike up Maketton Street, a two-way road with a grass median. Lined with new villas, modern apartment buildings, and vacant lots, it ran through an outlying suburb that twenty years earlier had been nothing but desert. All the buildings were new, and some of the bright shops looked inviting. But though the construction was just twenty years old, it looked a hundred.

Gait turned right into Number 9 Street and gunned his bike to power up the hill, swerving to avoid a bicyclist zigzagging in front of him with a tray of cakes balanced on his head. Number 9 climbed steeply to an overlook from which you could see all of Cairo, though today it was almost invisible in the heat haze.

The neighborhood was so new, nobody had bothered giving the streets names. Most just had numbers.

Gait stopped and leaned his motorbike against a spindly palm tree across from an impressive new nine-story building. Its windows were covered with green sunshades that made them look fortified. A logo adorned the facade: two crossed sabers on a green background, vaguely suggesting the Saudi flag, above an inscription in English and Arabic: "Muslim Brotherhood Headquarters." It had been inaugurated just a few months earlier.

Where they were once pursued by the authorities, the Brothers were now riding high. Hosni Mubarak was out of the way, and they hoped to be sharing power with the Egyptian Army after the coming elections. Polls suggested they would win at least 40 percent of the votes.

But behind the respectable facade of a peaceful and almost moderate political party lay an organization whose very existence the Brothers denied. Al-Tanzim al-Asasi was in charge of clandestine operations, partnering with radical Muslim movements in the neighboring countries, from Hamas to the Gaza radicals to the veterans of the Libyan Islamic Fighting Group. They venerated the name of Dr. Ayman al-Zawahiri, member of the Brotherhood, Egyptian agitator, once Osama bin Laden's right-hand man, and, since bin Laden's death, the head of al-Qaeda.

Gait entered a lobby guarded by a burly, bearded man in a sport shirt who greeted him with a respectful smile.

"Blessings upon you, brother. The others are waiting in Room 206."

Gait headed up the marble staircase, passing the portraits of the nine late leaders of the Brotherhood: austere bearded men, some of them wearing a fez.

The sign outside Room 206 read, "Islamic Social Services Bureau."

This was Al-Tanzim al-Asasi's cover. It did in fact deliver social services, but mainly as a way to gain new recruits. Inside, three men were seated at a table. Gait was offered a glass of mint tea. He played an important role in the organization, handling the Mukhabarat agents who fed information to the Brotherhood. They hoped that their favoring the Islamists would soon be rewarded. Besides, the Brothers were generous, padding the miserable pay of the officers who did their dirty work.

A man who went by the name Habib had the floor and gave Gait a broad smile.

"Did you get the information, brother?" he asked.

Gait nodded.

"Yes, thanks be to God. The man in Room 2621 of the Four Seasons Hotel is called Malko Linge. He is known to the Mukhabarat as an American agent working closely with the head of the CIA in Cairo. He arrived five days ago, but we don't know what he's doing here."

"Bravo!" said Habib. "You've done very well. Allah will reward you."

This meant that his services were no longer needed, and Gait left. Within minutes, he'd climbed on the little motorbike and headed downtown to his job in a *shawarma* restaurant.

This time, Malko wasn't even able to approach Cynthia. She was indeed at the hotel pool, but she was accompanied by her dark-skinned "shadow." They were sitting in folding chairs by their pool cabana, chatting and reading.

Malko had had no word from Jerry Tombstone, who said he would contact him in case anything new came up.

He watched as Cynthia stood up and dove into the pool, all eyes on her. She was wearing a black bathing suit whose top was so low it was almost indecent. Though of course at the Four Seasons they were practically in Europe.

The Brother who called himself Habib entered the Costa Café in Zamalek, the northern part of Gezira Island and one of Cairo's most expensive neighborhoods. There were several Costa Cafés in the city, and this one, at the corner of al-Maraashli and Taha Hussein Streets, was the most in vogue. With its skimpily dressed women patrons, it was the last place you would expect to see an Islamist.

Habib walked around a vendor reclining by a wall with a stack of oranges for sale, ignored a poster for iced coffees, and sat down at a table occupied by a man alone. Bearded, about thirty, wearing a shirt and jeans, he looked like an aging student.

The man greeted Habib warmly: "May the blessings of Allah be upon you, brother."

Habib respectfully returned the greeting to a man he knew only as "Shalubi." This was the head of Al-Tanzim al-Asasi for the Cairo region, and someone the Mukhabarat had never managed to identify. He worked as a secretary in a law firm, spoke perfect English, and led a quiet life with his four children and a cloistered wife, who of course never set foot outside the house.

He listened to Habib's story carefully, weighing it against what he already knew. Shalubi was the man who had set up the security cordon around Ibrahim al-Senussi, at Abu Bukatalla's request. Al-Tanzim al-Asasi couldn't say no to the Libyan Islamist, who had been furnishing the organization and its friends in Gaza with weapons since the start of the Libyan revolution. These included surface-to-air missiles, which had been impossible to obtain before.

So when Bukatalla asked Al-Tanzim al-Asasi to use one of the missiles they'd been given to shoot down a British Airways plane, no one raised any objection. And from the moment al-Senussi arrived in Cairo, Al-Tanzim al-Asasi agents had been observing his every action and passing the information to Libya.

Shalubi finished his ice cream and paid for it.

"I'll leave you now, brother," he said to Habib. "Your information is valuable. May Allah protect you."

The two men left the Café Costa and Shalubi headed off on foot. He distrusted taxis, preferring to use only public transit, as bus drivers rarely belonged to the Mukhabarat. He walked as far as Abu el Feda Street on the west side of the island before hailing a cab and giving the driver an address in Giza.

As the taxi slowly made its way across the 6th October Bridge, an east-west overpass above the island, Shalubi prayed to God for help in making the right decision. Oddly enough, he never felt a twinge of fear, yet any Mukhabarat agent would have ripped out all of a prisoner's fingernails just to learn his name.

When Shalubi reached the al-Sharabi neighborhood, he got out half a mile from his final destination, a tire-retreading shop at the rear of a courtyard. He crossed the workshop, ignored by the men laboring over their bald tires, and entered a small glassed-in office in the back. Its occupant hugged him, and they stepped into the next room. The workshop boss carefully rolled back a carpet, revealing a trapdoor in the floor, and opened it.

A metal ladder led to a huge cellar filled with a dense jumble of bric-a-brac and lit by neon lights.

At the sight of the two visitors, a thin man busy at a workbench straightened up. This was Abdul Gabal al-Afghani, who had fired the SAM at the British Airways plane.

He was using an electronic test bed to check a partly disassembled Strela. He embraced Shalubi, whom he deeply respected.

"Do you have a lot of work on your hands?" asked the Al-Tanzim al-Asasi chieftain.

"Yes, I do. Those are going to Gaza, and I want to make sure they're working properly."

Shalubi nodded.

"You're going to have to put that worthy task aside for a while," he said with a smile. "I have a job for you."

"If such is the will of God."

"It's dangerous."

"I'll do it," said al-Afghani, eager to make up for his failure in the attack on the British Airways 777.

"We must eliminate an enemy of God," Shalubi said solemnly.

His hand on his heart, al-Afghani promptly answered:

"If he is an enemy of God, he is my enemy as well."

"I'll tell you what's involved. It must be done quickly."

Shalubi had decided he couldn't allow a CIA agent near Ibrahim al-Senussi, especially since the man also knew the Libyan's lover. All infidel women were whores, so maybe she was his lover as well. Shalubi didn't know exactly what al-Senussi was doing in Cairo, but he clearly had to be protected from "pollution." So Shalubi had decided he would eliminate the CIA man without raising the issue with the Libyan Brothers. He was sure they would approve.

All he had to do was prepare the trap.

CHAPTER 7

Sprawled on a deck chair by the fifth-floor swimming pool, Malko tried to concentrate on the *Financial Times*, which predicted nothing but economic catastrophes in the coming weeks. The forced inactivity of this assignment was starting to weigh on him.

Jerry Tombstone's romantic gambit seemed to be stalled. He must have assumed that Malko could seduce every woman he met at a mere glance. Cynthia Mulligan was certainly gorgeous, and she seemed to find him attractive, but the young Brit was sticking awfully close to her Libyan shadow.

Just then, the two of them appeared. Al-Senussi was wearing a T-shirt and Bermuda shorts, Cynthia a pareo skirt slit up the side. As they made for their usual pool cabana, she shot Malko a quick look. It was nice for his self-esteem but not enough for his plan.

Back to the *Financial Times*.

The sun got hotter, and Malko was beginning to feel like a lobster in a pot of boiling water.

That morning, he'd had a short talk with Tombstone. In his calm, slow voice, the station chief reminded him that he had to be patient and that their business was important enough for the restless Austrian to hang in there. He also pointed out that being forced to loll in the sunshine in a palace was hardly a nightmare, whereas he was being constantly badgered by Langley, demanding updates.

The door to the hotel opened again. This time it was the couple Malko had seen the day before. The woman was still draped in her *niqab*, and her likely husband led her by the fingertips, looking as serious as a pope. There was no danger of them taking a dip in the pool. They ordered fruit juices and settled in.

It was now almost one o'clock. From time to time, Malko glanced toward the cabana where Cynthia and her lover sat relaxing in the shade of the canvas awning.

As he was watching, al-Senussi picked up his phone to answer a call. Malko couldn't hear what he was saying, and it was probably in Arabic, anyway.

The conversation was a short one. Al-Senussi put away his phone with a look of annoyance. Then he stood and put on his T-shirt, walked past Malko, and disappeared inside the hotel. Intrigued, Malko waited ten or fifteen minutes. When al-Senussi didn't reappear, he strolled over to the cabana.

"I'm not bothering you, am I?" he said. "Your friend . . ."

Cynthia was reading a magazine and looked up with a smile.

"He had to leave," she said. "An urgent meeting. He said he'd be away for a few hours."

Malko's pulse sped up.

"Didn't he want to take you with him?"

She smiled again.

"Oh no! He's going to some mosque way off in Giza. It's called al-Isti-something. Would you like to have a drink with me?"

Cynthia seemed as bored as he was.

Malko now had a dilemma. Should he stay with his assigned target, who was wearing a white Dior bikini so sexy it might have been designed by the devil himself, or follow up on al-Senussi's unexpected meeting? Duty called, alas.

"I'm sorry, but I have a meeting, too," he said with regret. "I hope you'll still be here when I return."

She gave him a meaningful look.

"In that case, hurry back," she said lightly.

"See you later, I hope," he said, striding off under the hot sun.

An ever-faithful sentry, Nasser was waiting in the Mercedes, and he jumped out when Malko approached. With his bushy eyebrows and Saddam Hussein mustache, he really does look scary, thought Malko. A human bulldog.

"Do you know a mosque in the Giza area called Isti-something?"

"Sure. The al-Istiqama, on Giza Square. It's very well known."

"Why's that?"

"Because it's Muslim Brotherhood territory."

"Did you see our 'client' go by?"

"Yeah, about five minutes ago. He took a taxi."

"All right, let's go to the mosque. Is it far?"

"If we make good time, a half hour, inshallah."

Malko didn't know if following al-Senussi would turn up anything useful, but the man's impromptu meeting intrigued him.

Karim Akhdar consulted his fake Rolex. The blond foreigner he'd been watching had left the hotel fifteen minutes earlier, following Ibrahim al-Senussi. Akhdar dialed a number, said a few words, and stowed the phone in his djellaba pocket.

"We're going home," he said to his wife. "It's getting hot."

His day's work was done.

"There's the mosque," Nasser said as they headed down a ramp to an open space with a kind of market and a bus terminal with a line of green buses. Beyond it, a small mosque stood next to a massive white telephone company building topped by a giant antenna.

Nasser parked by the telecom building and turned to Malko.

"Want me to see if I can find him?"

"No, I'll go myself."

Malko had noticed several other foreigners in a small crowd at the mosque's entrance and figured he wouldn't stand out too much. The building had a modest blue-and-white facade with a row of columns. A side entrance led to a hospital that the Muslim Brotherhood had built behind it.

A loudspeaker brayed a constant stream of prayers, interrupted with loud cries of "*Allahu akbar*."

And there were the money changers, right in front of the temple!

A young man was hawking stacks of prayer CDs under a big blue umbrella with an incongruous Nivea logo. Next to him, another man was selling socks and underwear. Yet another stand sold books. A few tourists were taking pictures under the watchful eyes of two hulking bearded men wearing djellabas and skullcaps, one white, the other brown.

They didn't exactly look like fans of representative democracy.

A little farther on, a dozen Egyptian soldiers in their pancake-flat red berets and GK bulletproof vests were guarding the mosque. Under the current government, the Muslim Brothers clearly had an inside track.

Malko paused, unsure what to do next. He didn't see al-Senussi anywhere, and the two big bearded men kept looking at him, clearly wary of infidels.

The one wearing the brown skullcap, who had glasses, came over with a smile, hand on his heart.

"Salaam alaikum," he said. "Are you interested in our activities? Are you a journalist?"

"Just a tourist," Malko assured him. "I'm out for a walk."

"If you are one of the People of the Book, you can visit the mosque."

Malko politely declined. While the bearded man was talking, a crowd of Arabs had gathered to listen.

"Are you the imam of the mosque?" Malko asked.

"Oh no, I don't have enough education for that," said the man with a modest smile. "I'm just a helper, eager to serve Allah."

The flood of words continued to pour from the loudspeakers overhead. It was both good-natured and scary: an unstoppable machine. These people's certainties are rock solid, thought Malko. They don't ever pass up a chance to proselytize.

"Come inside and visit the mosque," the bearded man repeated.

Malko yielded to his insistence. Led by his minder, he climbed the steps and took off his shoes at the entrance.

It was cool inside the mosque, with a lighted panel on the left announcing the schedule of the day's various prayers. A few men prayed or meditated, leaning against columns. One lay curled up on the floor, sound asleep, some poor soul who'd come to get out of the heat.

"Many people come to this mosque because of the hospital that we run next door," the big man whispered. "We do a lot of good work here. Would you like to visit the hospital?"

Malko politely declined.

Of al-Senussi, not a sign. Malko's trip had been a complete waste of time. He should've stayed by the pool and flirted with the lovely Cynthia.

He began to feel comfortable only after he got his shoes back on and was free of his minder.

There were more people in front of the mosque now, clustered around the open-air stands under the dull gaze of the soldiers. Malko walked down the steps toward them.

Abdul Gabal al-Afghani was lurking in the crowd, watching the mosque steps. His right hand gripped the horn handle of a long dagger he'd sharpened for the occasion.

He could have followed his victim into the mosque, but it was a grave sin to kill a man in the House of God. Even an infidel. And if nothing else, al-Afghani was a man of deep faith. It was the only thing that kept him going in this shitty life, where he worked like a dog for a few hundred Egyptian pounds. His only joy was getting his wife pregnant every year.

He gradually made his way toward the mosque. The foreigner had come down the steps and was mixing with the crowd.

Al-Afghani followed, every fiber of his being drawn taut toward his goal: accomplishing the will of God.

In moments, he was behind the man he had come to kill, who was headed for the telecommunications building. A few more steps and al-Afghani would be almost close enough to touch him. With a casual gesture, he drew the dagger from his djellaba pocket and laid it along his thigh. The crowd was so dense, nobody noticed. He had killed this way before, jamming the blade in the victim's kidneys, then yanking it out. If the knife got stuck, he left it in the wound.

This was a working-class neighborhood, and al-Afghani knew he would have no trouble losing himself in the crowd afterward. He had already spotted a little *shawarma* stand on the avenue above the mosque where he could lie low until the excitement died down.

He got still closer, his victim's back now just a few feet away.

Holding his dagger horizontally, he lunged. But habit was stronger than caution, and before striking he yelled, "*Allahu akbar!*" at the top of his lungs.

Startled by the scream, Malko spun around to find himself facing a bearded man with a beaked nose and wild eyes, thrusting a dagger at his stomach like a lance.

In a blur of motion, the swordsman slashed at his belly.

CHAPTER 8

Nasser kept an eye on Malko constantly, except for one brief period, when he went into the mosque. He was in no danger there, Nasser knew. In the Islamic world there are rules that are never broken, even in jihad.

When the Austrian came out, Nasser stayed in the crowd but eased closer to him. He was only a few yards away when he noticed a man shoving bystanders aside, apparently eager to get through. That caught the veteran cop's attention, and a moment later he spotted the long dagger the man was holding in his right hand down along his djellaba. Nasser pushed someone out of his way to get behind him. He wasn't armed, but his size gave him an advantage over the man with the dagger, who was now less than a yard from Malko.

Suddenly, everything happened at once. As al-Afghani reached out to stab his victim and gave his cry, "*Allahu akbar!*," Nasser sprang and grabbed him from behind.

The two men fell to the ground, struggling.

The would-be killer fought like the devil. He lost a sandal, tried to punch Nasser, then leaped to his feet, still holding his dagger. He had another chance to kill Malko, who was only a few feet away. But when he went to strike, Nasser slammed his wrist with a karate chop, making him drop his weapon.

One of the big bearded helpers was howling like an air-raid siren, yelling to the soldiers for help.

Al-Afghani fought his way free of the crowd and sprinted away, dodging between the buses in the terminal. Nasser tried to follow, but two soldiers grabbed him, thinking he was the attacker.

In shock, Malko stared at the dagger lying on the ground. It had almost gone into his belly. A voice at his ear made him jump.

"Are you hurt, brother?"

The tall helper with the brown skullcap was looking at him with concern.

"No, I'm okay," said Malko. "But I don't know why that man tried to stab me."

"He's a fanatic. Some people think infidels shouldn't be allowed in the mosques, that it's a sin. That's wrong, of course. You have to forgive them."

The soldiers had come over by now and were standing around, having released the Mukhabarat agent. In a loud voice, the tall helper ordered them back to their pointless guard duties. Then he took Malko by the elbow and said, "Come with me. A glass of tea will help settle your nerves."

He was holding Malko so tightly there was no point in arguing. The two of them climbed a few steps and entered a kind of sacristy. It was a hot, dusty cubicle with benches along the wall and a large repoussé copper tray on a stand. A boy appeared, and the bearded helper shouted something at him.

He came back moments later with two glasses of sweetened tea.

Malko took a sip, grateful to relieve his thirst. But his brain was in a whirl, and he was furious.

By mentioning this meeting, sweet Cynthia Mulligan had cold-bloodedly sent him to his death! But then Malko caught himself, ashamed of his suspicions. For her to do that, she would have had to know where the meeting was, which wasn't likely. And she couldn't have expected Malko to go chasing after her lover.

One thing was clear, however: someone who knew who Malko was had counted on his doing just that. A clever gambit, and it very nearly worked.

Malko set down his glass.

"Thank you for your kindness," he said, standing up.

"Please come back whenever you like," said the bearded man, without a hint of irony.

Outside, the crowd had dispersed, the soldiers were in the shade again, and the dagger that had nearly killed him had vanished. Malko walked over to find the Mercedes empty. Looking around, he realized Nasser had disappeared. The keys were in the ignition, but Malko didn't feel up to driving in Cairo. Besides, he was sure to get lost.

Malko took out his cell phone and called him.

The Mukhabarat agent was standing in front of a store window full of shoes, across the street from a chicken and lamb *shawarma* stand. A single customer was at the counter: Malko's attacker.

It was Nasser's doggedness as a cop that helped him find the man, and even then, it was almost by accident. Once the soldiers released him, he ran in the direction the fleeing man had gone, taking the stairs beyond the bus terminal up to busy Sharia el-Aram.

He found himself in a dense crowd, unsure what to do next. The man he was chasing was probably long gone, he thought. Just the same, he decided to walk as far as a bus stop a few hundred yards away; Islamists often used public transit, he knew.

It was while walking down the sidewalk that Nasser spotted the man he was after. He was at a *shawarma* stand, calmly having a bite to eat!

Nasser immediately stationed himself on the other side of the street. He stayed hidden in the crowd, determined to follow him.

Just then his cell phone rang.

Recognizing Malko's voice, Nasser said:

"I found the man who tried to kill you, and I'm following him. You can take a taxi back to the hotel."

By his fourth glass of tea, Ibrahim al-Senussi was seething with impatience. The man who had called him at the Four Seasons when he was with Cynthia was the same Nabil who had first taken him to meet Abu Bukatalla. On the phone he'd been terse as usual, merely telling him where to meet: in front of the al-Istiqama mosque on Giza Square. But this time he'd added that it was urgent.

Sure that this involved preparation for his trip to Libya, al-Senussi didn't hesitate.

When they met, Nabil immediately led him up to Sharia al-Aram, where they took a taxi to the Ramses Railway Station.

They sat down in a small café, and Nabil explained that they were expecting someone who was coming from Marsa Matruh.

But the wait went on and on. Nabil kept phoning, then hanging up in disappointment.

"He hasn't arrived yet," he said.

Al-Senussi tried to make the best of it, while wondering how soon he could get back to the hotel.

Deep in thought, Malko watched absently as his taxi drove past gritty, crowded streets. Somebody now knew what he was doing in Cairo and had decided to kill him. That news might ruffle even Jerry Tombstone's Olympian calm.

As his taxi pulled up in front of the Four Seasons, Malko could still see the wild eyes of the unknown man who had tried to stab him, and hear his scream ringing in his ears.

At least there was no mistaking the style of the crime.

The chill of the air-conditioned lobby did him good. Without thinking, he headed for the elevators and was about to push the button for his floor when he suddenly pushed number 5 instead.

Malko didn't know if al-Senussi had come back to the hotel or if Cynthia Mulligan would still be by the pool. At the worst, he could have a vodka to help him unwind. The area around the pool was empty, but al-Senussi's cabana wasn't closed. Some things lay scattered on a low table between the two folding chairs.

He walked over to the cabana and called:

"Cynthia?"

"Who is it?" came her voice from inside.

Malko pushed aside the changing-room curtain and found

himself nose to nose with the young Englishwoman. She was bending over to pick up her sunglasses and unwittingly offering her breasts as if on a tray.

Cynthia stood up, and their eyes met. It was like an electric shock. Malko was swept by an irresistible impulse. The shadow of death was still hovering around him. He'd come close to dying, which always sparked a rush of adrenaline in him and an intense hunger for life.

Cynthia was staring at him, not sure what to do.

Without a word, he cupped her breasts in his hands as if they were fruit. She was wearing only her two-piece Dior suit, and she exuded sensuality from every pore. In the blink of an eye he had her pressed against the wooden wall of the cabana, his tongue forcing her teeth apart in a furious kiss.

He had released the young woman's breasts and was now stroking her through the bathing suit, his fingers on her soft, warm vulva. His cock was so stiff, it would have done a young stud proud. He'd stopped thinking, even put Cynthia's lover out of his mind, though he might appear at any moment.

Their confused embrace lasted a few seconds. Cynthia seemed stunned by this whirlwind of lust. Then suddenly Malko felt the young woman's tongue playing with his own. She had moved from resistance to collaboration.

She wrapped her arms around his neck and pushed her hips to his.

It was all Malko needed.

He feverishly stripped off his alpaca trousers and shoved his underpants aside, freeing a penis that felt ready to explode.

Not to be outdone, Cynthia slid the bottom of her bathing suit down her long legs, revealing a trimmed, heart-shaped bush. Malko slid his fingers into her, but the young Brit lightly pushed him away, instead leading him to what looked like a cot. Putting her hands on his shoulders, she forced him to lie down on his back. Not a word had been said. It was pure sex.

Cynthia straddled Malko as if she were mounting a horse and pressed herself against him. Then she slowly began to move back and forth, masturbating him with her pussy. Malko expected her to lift herself so he could enter her, but she had other ideas. He was so hard by now, it was painful.

Cynthia calmly unbuttoned Malko's shirt and skillfully stroked his chest, lingering over his nipples. Malko hastened to undo the top of her bathing suit.

Leaning over him, Cynthia continued to rub his penis. Suddenly she spoke for the first time.

"Grab my ass with both hands," she growled.

He did so, and she rocked back and forth faster. With his erection pressed against Cynthia's pussy, Malko could feel an orgasm rising. As he squeezed the mounds of her ass harder, she spoke again.

"I love your holding me like that," she murmured, and moaned softly.

Malko tried to lift her up so he could penetrate her, but she was too heavy.

Unable to restrain himself, he suddenly came, all over his belly.

The look in Cynthia's eyes had changed, becoming darker, more intense. Abruptly she lifted herself a bit, and, still astride him, scooted up until her crotch was level with Malko's face. Then she lowered herself onto his lips.

"How about you take care of me now?" she asked sweetly.

Poised above him, chest erect, she trembled when Malko's tongue began to explore her. She started moving slightly, giving little cries to encourage him. She seemed incredibly receptive to his caresses.

Cynthia had her hands on her breasts and was playing with them, stroking her nipples, eyes closed. When he stuck a finger into her anus, she shuddered but didn't protest.

Little by little, Malko got more involved in this unexpected game. He put more energy into his caresses and could feel her start each time his tongue brushed a sensitive spot. Gradually, the young woman's attitude began to change. She wasn't playing anymore, but surrendering to pleasure.

Her hips gave a sudden thrust and she shoved her pussy against Malko's mouth. Then she slowly eased herself forward.

He had another erection by now, but Cynthia paid no attention. Instead she gave him a mischievous look.

"I had no idea you could use your tongue so well."

That was clearly the kind of erotic play she enjoyed.

Feeling a little frustrated, Malko wanted to lift her so he could slip inside her, but she pushed him gently away.

"You have to get out of here. He could come back at any minute."

It was the voice of reason. Malko put on his pants as Cynthia slipped back into her bathing suit. When he pulled the curtain aside, she was freshening her makeup. She paused.

"Will you be in Cairo a little longer?" she asked.

"I think so, yeah."

"So much the better," she said with a smile. "My boyfriend has to go to Libya. I was thinking of going with him, but it would be a pity not to take advantage of your talents. What room are you in?"

"Suite 2621."

"I'll call you as soon as I'm free."

The curtain fell back.

Malko went inside the hotel, still feeling a bit stunned by what had just happened. In any case, he had a valuable piece of information: Ibrahim al-Senussi was headed for Libya. Jerry Tombstone's plan appeared to be working, though not quite the way he'd expected.

The moment he got back to his room, he phoned the CIA station chief. Tombstone hardly seemed surprised when Malko said he had a lot of things to tell him.

"I'll pick you up and take you to dinner at one of the few good Egyptian restaurants in town."

No sooner had Malko hung up when his cell rang again. It was Nasser.

"I'm back," said the Mukhabarat agent. "I followed your attacker, and I know where he's hiding."

Malko could feel his pulse start to race. This was more than he could have hoped for. Nasser really was good.

"Where is he?"

"He went into a tire-retreading shop in a working-class neighborhood called al-Sharabi. I staked out the place for more than two hours. The shop closed and some workers came out, but the guy didn't. I think he's hiding there."

"You sure they didn't spot you?"

"Positive."

It would be hard to investigate there without attracting attention. But if they could interrogate the man, they might find out who had ordered him to kill Malko.

"I'll tell Mr. Tombstone about it. Meanwhile, keep the information to yourself."

Nasser swore he would be as silent as the tombs of Luxor, but that hardly reassured Malko. The driver's first loyalty had to be to the Mukhabarat.

Things were starting to heat up. Malko wondered if al-Senussi had returned from his mysterious meeting, but he didn't dare call the couple's suite to check. Besides, he was having dinner with Jerry Tombstone. He had a lot to tell him.

Ibrahim al-Senussi was in a foul mood. After they'd hung around the Ramses Railroad Station for nearly two hours, Nabil had been forced to recognize that the person they were going to meet must have changed his plans. He hoped the next meeting to set al-Senussi's departure would be the right one.

Back at the hotel, al-Senussi found Cynthia relaxing in a bubble bath. She seemed in a very good mood and wasn't even bothered by his abrupt disappearance.

"Let's have dinner at the Cairo Tower," he suggested. "They say there's a beautiful view from the top."

"A beautiful view of this lousy town?" she asked, pouting. "I'd be surprised."

Al-Senussi didn't argue. He was wrestling with a different problem: whether he should alert the Cairo MI6 representative about his going to Libya.

He helped himself to a scotch from the minibar and tried to relax.

Cynthia unwittingly helped distract him when she came out of the dressing room a little later. Made up like the queen of Sheba, she was wearing one of those figure-hugging silk dresses she liked.

"Let's go, love!" she said cheerfully.

Things weren't all gloom and doom.

Tombstone and Malko were practically the only diners on the Sofitel terrace by the river.

Blue eyes narrowed in concentration, the CIA man listened as Malko described his afternoon. When he reached the murder attempt, Tombstone exclaimed:

"God, you were lucky! But it's strange. The al-Istiqama mosque is a Brotherhood base, all right, but I can't see them attacking you at this point."

"No one could have known that I would follow Ibrahim," said Malko. "Not even Cynthia. It could only be a plan hatched by people who don't want me close to him. Probably the same ones who tried to shoot down his plane with the Strela.

"It was a trap, and it wouldn't have worked if I hadn't gone to the mosque—though in that case I wouldn't have found out about it. I think the killers are still watching al-Senussi. They tried to eliminate me, and they'll try again."

The *mezzes* came, and Tombstone tore into them hungrily. When he'd had his fill of hummus and dolmas, he asked:

"So you don't know where al-Senussi went?"

"I don't have the slightest idea," admitted Malko. "Just as we don't know who he met in Marsa Matruh. But people are aware that I'm working for the Agency."

"Is that all?"

"No, it isn't," said Malko in a neutral tone. "My relationship with Cynthia has moved to the next level."

The American's handsome blue eyes took on an almost salacious gleam.

"You slept with her?"

"That's one way of putting it."

"I won't ask you for the details," said Tombstone, whose avid expression suggested he was dying to.

Malko picked at a stuffed grape leaf.

"It was happenstance," he said. "She was feeling unsatisfied. You could call it a simple sexual impulse, a momentary lapse. She's bored, and I don't think she's in love with al-Senussi."

"Bit of a slut, isn't she?"

Malko smiled. "You're being too hard on her. Women often act on complicated motives."

"Anyway, well done!" approved Tombstone. "You've carried out the first part of your assignment."

Then he sighed.

"You're lucky to be able to seduce a woman as beautiful as Cynthia Mulligan. It's never happened to me."

"Thanks to the 'slut,' I've learned something interesting," said Malko. "Al-Senussi is planning to go to Libya, and he wants to take her along."

"Now, that's news!" said Tombstone, cheering up. "And it would explain the attempt to kill you. They don't want you following him. What's he going to do in Libya? And when is he leaving?"

"She didn't tell me, and she probably doesn't know."

Silence fell, broken by the blaring loudspeaker on a tourist boat.

After mopping up the last of the *mezzes*, Tombstone looked across the table at Malko.

"You have to take your relationship with Cynthia to the next level," he said. "And if they go to Libya, follow them."

"That won't be easy. They know me."

"We'll see. I'll talk to the MI6 cousins tomorrow and find out if al-Senussi told them about this trip. If he hasn't, that means we also have to be wary of him. He's keeping some things from us.

"You know, this trip surprises me. Al-Senussi told MI6 in London that he didn't want to go to Libya right now, that it was risky. Wanted to wait a while before stating his intentions. He planned to have his old supporters come to Cairo first.

"At that point, we could launch Operation Sunrise: introduce al-Senussi as a credible figure with a historic background to represent the new Libya. Of course, for that to work, we have to keep him alive."

Tombstone thirstily downed half his Strella beer.

Malko had saved the best for last.

"I think you should give Nasser a bonus," he said. "Not only did he save my life, but he says he found the man who tried to kill me."

When he described Nasser's phone call, Malko expected Tombstone to jump for joy. That didn't happen.

"Shit, shit, shit!" swore the CIA man. "I hope he hasn't gone and blabbed about this."

Tombstone already had his phone out and was dialing a number.

Then he shook his head, looking disappointed.

"He isn't answering. I just pray he hasn't told his agency. As brutal as they are, the Mukhabarat could react like a bull in a china shop. I'll phone General Mowafi first thing in the morning."

A felucca silently glided by, sailing down the Nile—a classic, postcard-perfect image of Egypt. But then a singer, covered from neck to ankles in a black dress, planted herself in front of a nearby microphone and started belting out a song.

"Let's get out of here," said Tombstone. "This business with Nasser worries me. It's too soon to take action. We want to roll up the whole network."

At that very moment, Nasser Ihab was in a cramped office in the Mukhabarat's Rasiqa Avenue headquarters, typing on his computer. There was no air-conditioning and the place was stifling. Nasser was starving and eager to get home to his wife, but he had to follow an absolutely mandatory daily rule: file a report on the day he'd spent in the CIA's service. That was the price of being allowed to pocket two salaries: one as a Mukhabarat agent, the other in the cash bonuses he got from the Agency.

Nasser's fingers paused in the air when it came to explaining how he had run Malko's attacker to ground. If he kept it quiet and his bosses found out, he might have real problems, maybe even find himself without a job.

In the end, he told the whole story in detail. Then he signed the report, dropped it in a box in the hallway, and went out to the Mercedes. He secretly hoped to get a bonus for this information, whose ins and outs he didn't fully understand.

Cynthia was eating breakfast with al-Senussi, as she did every morning. The Libyan went down to work out in the gym, but not before making enthusiastic use of her body. Again, this was something that happened every morning, and even though she was bisexual, Cynthia enjoyed it. There was something very exciting about being drilled like an oil well while still half asleep.

Al-Senussi was buttering a croissant when she broke the silence.

"When are you leaving for Libya?"

"I don't know yet. Why?"

"I've been thinking about it, and I think I'm going to stay in Cairo."

Al-Senussi felt a wave of relief: he wouldn't be risking offending his Libyan friends after all. He hid his satisfaction behind a show of disappointment.

"That's too bad," he said. "You sure?"

"Yes. I looked at a guidebook, and I saw there are plenty of things to do here. Besides, I think the trip might be tiring. There are probably loads of mosquitoes there."

As she talked, Cynthia was thinking of the man who had given her such a delicious orgasm. By staying in Cairo, she could hope for many more.

Al-Senussi feigned reluctance.

"You'll be good, won't you? Women like you are as rare as hen's teeth here."

"I have no intention of getting myself an Egyptian boyfriend."

Which was technically true.

"Okay, fine," said the Libyan. "I'll tell you when I'm leaving. But there isn't much for me to bring back for you from my country, unfortunately."

"That's all right," she said, standing up to get more croissants.

As he watched her go, al-Senussi reflected that Cynthia really did have a beautiful rump.

Fathi el-Said, the owner of the retreading shop, felt his stomach tighten when three military police vehicles pulled up in front of his workshop. Men in red berets and GK bulletproof vests jumped out and took positions in the narrow street.

He was still clinging to a faint hope when an agent burst into his workshop and slammed him against the wall.

"Where's the son of a bitch hiding?" the man screamed, shoving the barrel of his AK-47 into el-Said's belly.

El-Said was mute with terror. The agents were already storming through the shop, manhandling his three workers. Swinging fists and gun butts, they forced them to lie down on the floor.

Then an officer came in, pistol in hand, glaring. He jammed the gun into el-Said's neck and roared:

"You're hiding a terrorist. Where is he?"

It took el-Said a few seconds to find his voice.

"I'm not hiding anybody, *sidi*," he croaked. "You can check. I'm an honest Muslim and I don't know any terrorists."

They forced him to his knees, and the Mukhabarat officer, a captain named Saadi, went to the back of the shop. The three workers' papers were in order, and he quickly decided they hadn't done anything wrong. He returned to el-Said.

"One of my men saw a killer come in here yesterday afternoon. Where is he?"

"I don't know about any killer, *sidi*, I swear on the Quran. There's nobody here. What's his name?"

Saadi, who didn't know the suspect's name, kicked him in the stomach.

"You're a liar!" he roared. "Tell us who this man is and where he is, and we'll let you go."

"By Allah, I swear I don't know what you're talking about."

"Have it your way," said the officer. "We're going to search the place, and if you're lying, I'll kill you with my own hands."

More soldiers crowded into the workshop and started searching. It didn't take long; the place was small. El-Said was counting the minutes and praying to God. Suddenly an agent in the little office kicked the carpet aside, revealing a corner of the trapdoor.

With a yell, they rushed in and rolled up the carpet, uncovering the trapdoor. The captain grabbed el-Said by the collar and hauled him into the office.

"What the hell is this?" he roared.

"It leads to a storage area. There's nothing down there but junk and old tires."

Two soldiers had already raised the trapdoor. The basement was very dark. Flashlight in hand, one started down the wooden steps. He was halfway down when a burst of gunfire from below rang out and he pitched forward.

Other soldiers rushed down in turn.

"Capture that dog alive!" yelled the captain.

A live prisoner is worth more than a corpse.

The first soldier had just reached the basement floor when it was rocked by a violent explosion—a sheet of yellow flame and smoke, then silence. Saadi, who'd been leaning over the trap, was thrown against the wall. Stunned for a few seconds, he rushed over and grabbed the shop owner by the throat, smashing his face with his pistol and swearing at him.

El-Said slumped to the floor, and Saadi kept hitting him. But when the shop owner stopped moving, the officer realized that he was more useful alive than dead. To his men, he yelled:

"Take this dog outside. I'll deal with him later."

Two soldiers cautiously descended the steps again. They stumbled over the bodies of their comrades as they groped though thick, acrid smoke. In addition to the two corpses, they found the body of a man who had blown himself up with a grenade.

Firefighters and ambulances were on their way. The neighborhood had been sealed off.

Leaving his men in place, the captain raced back to Mukhabarat headquarters. In the back of his pickup truck, two soldiers were sitting on el-Said, who was still unconscious.

A half hour later, the pickup passed the machine-gun emplacement that guarded the entrance to the Mukhabarat. Then it drove to a windowless gray cement building, the interrogation center.

In a basement room, el-Said was shackled to a metal chair welded to the floor. The room was soundproofed so the screams of prisoners being interrogated wouldn't disturb the work of the bureaucrats on the ground floor.

In Egypt, torture was a practice as old as the pharaohs.

Captain Saadi was preparing his equipment when his phone rang. A Mukhabarat agent at the shop said they had finally cleared the basement and found the unrecognizable body of the man who had blown himself up, as well as eight Russian surface-to-air missiles, still in their crates.

This was the most important seizure they'd made in a long time, and Saadi knew it could belong to only one organization: the Muslim Brotherhood's Al-Tanzim al-Asasi. And just one person could help him write a complete report: Fathi el-Said, the owner of the tire-retreading shop.

The Mukhabarat officer carefully fitted a medium bit into his drill and sat down on a stool facing the chair el-Said was chained to. The shop owner had regained consciousness and was now very sorry he hadn't been killed.

The Mukhabarat officer looked at him.

"Who's the guy who blew himself up, you cur?"

He didn't answer, so Saadi set the drill bit against the prisoner's left knee. El-Said screamed in terror.

"*Yallahs*," said the officer, pulling the trigger.

The drill bit instantly cut into skin and cartilage, sending out a spray of blood, some of which spattered the torturer. Saadi stopped for a few seconds.

"I'm going to drill as many holes as it takes to get you to tell the truth, dog."

When the prisoner eventually talked, Captain Saadi would know where the surface-to-air missiles had come from and where they were bound. He would also know the identity of the man who had committed suicide rather than let himself be captured.

CHAPTER 10

The secret meeting was held in a rarely used building in Nasr City. Shalubi, the Cairo head of the Brotherhood underground, had called an urgent meeting of his men. Thanks to a disposable SIM card, they would also be talking with Abu Bukatalla, who had just arrived in Marsa Matruh to pick up Ibrahim al-Senussi for his trip to Libya.

Shalubi looked grim. The Mukhabarat raid on Fathi el-Said's tire shop had been a terrible blow. Not only had they lost the Strelas—and they wouldn't get replacements anytime soon—but the Jund Ansar Allah had paid for them in advance. Shalubi had also lost one valuable man, Abdul Gabal al-Afghani, and probably a second, Fathi el-Said. Worst of all, the Mukhabarat might be able to work its way up the Al-Tanzim al-Asasi chain of command. If so, the Muslim Brothers could wind up paying a heavy political price.

The Brotherhood was keeping a low profile until the elections. Having to explain why its armed branch was in possession of surface-to-air missiles would be extremely awkward.

For the time being, however, that fact was still secret. Neither TV, nor press, nor radio had reported what had happened. The official story was that an oxygen tank had accidentally exploded in a workshop. Nobody in the neighborhood was likely to tell reporters about the presence of the Mukhabarat agents.

One of the men handed Shalubi the cell phone, saying:

"Our Libyan brother is on the line."

Abu Bukatalla, who knew what had happened at the tire shop, didn't hide his fury. He started by raking Shalubi over the coals, first, for deciding to kill the CIA agent without alerting him, and second, for failing. Ibrahim al-Senussi was due to travel to Libya and the CIA agent wasn't likely to follow, said Abu Bukatalla, so there was no problem. And in case the man did come, it would be easier to kill him in Libya than in Egypt.

Abu Bukatalla was an important person, and Shalubi didn't argue.

"I don't want to stay in Marsa Matruh much longer," the *takfiri* continued. "Al-Senussi must join me here, tonight. Don't call to tell him. Send Nabil to the Four Seasons."

"It will be done," said Shalubi, happy to have the Libyan prince off his hands.

"Take steps to make sure he isn't followed," said Abu Bukatalla. "Call me back at this number when everything is set."

"Those assholes!"

Jerry Tombstone was sputtering with rage when Malko entered his office. The CIA station chief had summoned him an hour earlier, and Malko had made his way through the various barriers protecting the American embassy.

"What's going on?" he asked.

"The Mukhabarat raided the place where the guy who tried to kill you was hiding, and it was a massacre: he blew himself up. They found Strelas in the basement, which proves that the British Airways attack and the attempt on you were committed by the same people: the Al-Tanzim al-Asasi. But not for their own account; they were working for the Libyans. We've got to find out who."

"So what do we do?"

"Stay close to al-Senussi. We can't let him slip through our fingers. It's for his own safety; I don't think he realizes the risks he's taking. And I don't like this trip to Libya one bit. I'm going to see General Mowafi at the Mukhabarat. His people have kicked over the anthill, and God knows what's going to happen next.

"At least we've identified the people who tried to shoot down al-Senussi's plan. We might be able to pick up a lead."

Al-Senussi had been exercising in the hotel gym and was just stepping out of the shower when somebody knocked on the door of his suite. Thinking it was room service, he opened it promptly, to find Nabil standing there. The young Egyptian stepped into the suite.

"I've come to get you," he announced. "We're leaving for Marsa Matruh."

"Right away?"

"That's right. I'm going with you. A car's waiting for us."

"Why right now?"

"I don't know," answered Nabil with a disarming smile.

Al-Senussi realized he would have to do as he said. Anyway, he didn't mind moving up his departure.

"All right, I'll get ready," he said. "You can wait for me downstairs."

Nabil didn't budge.

"I'd rather wait for you here," he said shyly but firmly.

Al-Senussi didn't argue. He thanked his lucky stars that he'd earlier paid a call on Herbert Mallows, the MI6 man in Cairo, to tell him about his upcoming trip to Libya. The Briton warned al-Senussi about the pitfalls that might await him on the other side of the border. He also approved his wish to meet General Younes. Finally, he gave al-Senussi a Thuraya satellite phone so he could stay in communication. Regular phones worked very poorly in Libya, if at all.

Al-Senussi quickly packed a suitcase and tried to phone Cynthia, who had gone to visit the Cairo museum.

No answer.

He tried four more times and then gave up, as Nabil grew visibly nervous. Resentfully, al-Senussi followed the young man out of the hotel and down to the street.

A car was waiting for them some distance down the Corniche el-Nil: an old Japanese model with a bearded man at the wheel. After driving a few hundred yards, the man turned left into a narrow street. To al-Senussi's surprise, a brick wall blocked the entire street a little farther on.

"You went the wrong way," he told Nabil.

"No, we didn't."

When they reached the wall, the car stopped and Nabil opened the door.

"Come with me," he said.

When al-Senussi got out, he realized there was a narrow opening between the brick wall and one of the buildings. The two men took this pedestrian passageway, with Nabil carrying al-Senussi's suitcase. An old gray Volkswagen Golf awaited them on the other side and took off as soon as they were seated. No one could be following them now. Al-Senussi, who wasn't familiar with the technique of ditching a car that might be tailing you, was a little confused.

After a while, they merged with the insane late-afternoon traffic and headed for the Ring Road to pick up the Alexandria highway. The car smelled of onions and trash. Al-Senussi suddenly regretted agreeing to the trip.

He would have done better to stay with Cynthia.

"Are you free for dinner tonight?" Cynthia Mulligan's joyful voice came over the house phone.

Malko couldn't believe his ears. He'd gone looking for the young woman at the pool, but the cabana was locked.

"Sure, but what about you?"

She laughed.

"He took off a while ago as if he had the devil on his tail. I wasn't even at the hotel. He just left me a message."

Clearly, she couldn't have cared less.

Malko's brain started to race. Was al-Senussi's sudden departure somehow connected with that morning's Mukhabarat action? He absolutely had to alert Jerry Tombstone.

"I'm free, all right," he told her.

"Okay, let's meet downstairs at nine o'clock."

"Aren't you worried about the hotel staff gossiping?"

"Nah, I doubt they care what the foreigners do," she said. "See you later."

Malko grabbed his cell phone.

It was a few moments before Tombstone answered.

"I'm at the Mukhabarat," said the CIA man. "Can we talk later?"

"Certainly. I just wanted to tell you that our friend left on his trip an hour ago."

"Do you know how?"

"No."

"Okay. I'll call you back later."

The Volkswagen was now beyond El Alamein, and night had fallen. They were driving slowly because of heavy truck traffic in both directions.

Nabil turned to al-Senussi.

"We're about halfway to Marsa Matruh," he said. "Would you like to stop for a cup of coffee?"

"No, thanks."

What he really wanted to do was to get there so he could phone Cynthia. He was angry that he hadn't been able to talk to her before leaving.

The highway stretched ahead of them, running as straight as an arrow along the coast. The sea to the right, the desert to the left. From time to time, the lights of a village or a gas station.

The Libyan tried to relax. He was starting to realize that becoming king was harder than he'd thought.

Malko was leaning on the railing of the ground-floor tearoom near the piano player when Cynthia stepped out of the elevator.

She looked so beautiful, it took his breath away.

She was wearing a black suit with narrow stripes. The skirt was split in front and went perfectly with her black "anti-mosquito" stockings. As she came closer, Malko noticed she was wearing a see-through black chiffon blouse over a lacy black bra.

With the jacket buttoned, she was perfectly decent. But with it open, she was something else again.

"Where are you taking me for dinner?" she asked, her eyes sparkling. "Someplace civilized, I hope."

"Let's try the Shepherd. It's a little way down the corniche."

"Is your driver here?"

Nasser hadn't come. He was probably feeling bad about what had happened.

"No, he isn't. We'll take one of the hotel's limos."

Looking as regal as Queen Nefertiti, Cynthia walked across the lobby, followed by hungry looks from the staff.

When they were in the limo, Malko's cell rang: Jerry Tombstone.

"I'm on my way to dinner with a lady friend," Malko said warningly. "What's new?"

"They took a man alive and interrogated him," said Tombstone. "He claims the Strelas were bound for Gaza, and he doesn't know anything about any attack, either on you or on the plane."

"Who are these people?"

"The armed branch of the Brotherhood, apparently. I asked the Mukhabarat to watch the Sallum border crossing. It's the only one open to Libya, so we should know when our friend crosses and who he's with."

"Fine," said Malko. "I'll call you tomorrow."

Cynthia was starting to give him quizzical looks. Fortunately, they had reached their destination.

The Shepherd was a shadow of its former self, alas. The

nightclub, which had once featured the best belly dancers in the Middle East, was closed, and the dining room was half empty.

Malko was on the verge of leaving, but he knew there were practically no other restaurants left in Cairo outside of the hotels. The offerings included the same old *mezzes*, plus some very tired-looking lamb. They fell back on the wine, which at least was fairly drinkable.

As the limo brought them back to the Four Seasons, Cynthia rested her head on Malko's shoulder and sighed.

"It's so nice to kick back and relax," she said.

"Didn't your boyfriend call?"

"He may have, but I turned off my phone. I want to be left alone tonight."

When they took the elevator, she pushed the button for the twenty-seventh floor. "In case he calls, I'd better be there to answer," she said.

If she were any more of a slut, it would kill her.

Malko opened her suit jacket and brushed the firm tip of one breast.

Cynthia closed her eyes with pleasure.

"If you stroke me very gently, you can make me come."

He wasn't able to; the elevator trip was too short. But the moment they reached her suite, he took up where he'd left off.

Cynthia got rid of her jacket and let him caress her, while gently stroking Malko's head. She started breathing faster, eyes closed, and suddenly a long sigh escaped her lips. When she looked at him, her eyes were dewy.

"You did it. You really have a magic touch."

Malko was a bit rougher when he put his hand through the slit in her skirt to find a pair of satin panties. He stroked them softly and soon had Cynthia practically purring.

She helped him slip the silky triangle down her long legs. Then, without taking off her black skirt, she turned around and kneeled at the edge of the bed. She tugged the skirt up over her hips, baring her bottom. Malko came closer.

"Do whatever you feel like," she said sweetly.

Marko's erection could have led an army. Without bothering to take off his pants, he freed his cock and approached the young woman. With her rear end thrust out and her back arched, Cynthia waited like a she-cat in heat.

Malko entered her in one thrust, going as deep as he could, then seized her hips and started a long in-and-out movement.

He slid smoothly in her soft, warm sheath, and Cynthia gave little flicks of her hips, as if to spur his desire. With her skirt pulled over her hips, black stockings far up her thighs, and high heels, she was charming, crude, and irresistible. Malko savored all this fully before exploding deep in her belly.

Cynthia let herself slide slowly forward until she was lying facedown on the bed. She hadn't come this time but seemed to be feeling good. Malko was still deep inside her.

"Are you satisfied?" she asked.

"Absolutely."

He pulled out and she rolled over onto her back. She undid her blouse, revealing a silent plea from her stiff nipples.

They were as hard as pencil tips, and when Malko's mouth closed around them, he could feel Cynthia shiver. Eyes half closed, she responded hungrily to his caresses. Then, with her skirt still hiked up, she slowly parted her legs, offering herself to him.

Malko couldn't ignore this second silent plea. As his head slipped between the young woman's thighs, she squeezed them together lightly, as if to greet him.

Her pussy was hot, and she immediately started responding to his caresses, much more actively than when he had penetrated her. Grabbing Malko's hair, she pressed his head against her crotch.

This got Malko so excited, he outdid himself.

Until Cynthia gave a hoarse cry, suddenly straightening her legs.

It really was her thing.

After some time had passed, she stood up, her eyes glazed.

"Want to take a shower?" she asked.

"You go first."

She stepped out of her skirt and stockings and headed for the bathroom, staggering slightly. Malko waited until he heard the water running before getting up in turn. The CIA wasn't paying him just to satisfy a supermodel. He walked over to a desk covered with some papers.

A sheet of hotel stationery immediately caught his eye. It bore a few lines in Arabic followed by telephone number.

A number that began with 218.

A Libyan number.

Malko took the paper, folded it, and put it in his pants pocket. He had just gotten back to the bed when Cynthia emerged from the bathroom wearing a robe. She stretched out next to him.

"Would you like to sleep here?" she offered.

Politely, Malko turned her down. He was eager to give Jerry Tombstone what might be the name and phone number of the person who had tried to shoot down Ibrahim al-Senussi and dozens of other innocent people.

Including the delectable Cynthia Mulligan.

CHAPTER 11

Jerry Tombstone's office was so quiet, you could have heard a pin drop. One of the embassy's Arab linguists was bent over his desk, studying the note Malko had taken from Cynthia Mulligan's room. He wrote a few words on a piece of paper and handed it to the CIA station chief.

"It's the number of a Libyan cell phone," he said. "But there's no way to know who it belongs to."

His job done, the translator left the office.

Tombstone looked disappointed.

"Let's see if the number appears in Abu Bukatalla's file," he said, turning on his computer.

He typed the code that gave him access to the CIA's top-secret list of Islamists. A series of names scrolled by, and the screen stopped on the photograph of a fierce-looking bearded man. Tombstone leaned closer to examine the text by the photo, with Malko reading over his shoulder.

It was very enlightening.

Abu Bukatalla hailed from the eastern Libyan town of

Derna, a jihadist hotbed. He'd been the regional head of the Libyan Islamic Fighting Group, an anti-Qaddafi group with ties to al-Qaeda that had carried out violent actions against the regime for years. Abu Bukatalla then traveled to Iraq to fight the Americans and in 2003 was arrested in Fallujah and sent to Guantanamo, where he spent the next four years. He was released in 2007 because it was determined that he hadn't committed any crimes against the United States in Iraq.

On the other hand, a note indicated that while at Guantanamo, he had become even more radical, embracing the *takfiri* cause.

Handed over to the Libyan authorities, Abu Bukatalla spent a few months in jail and was released after swearing an oath that he had given up activism.

A big gap in his résumé followed, until March 2011, when he emerged as the head of the Abu Salim Brigade, a Benghazi-based militia. Not much was known about his activities, or even the location of his base in Libya. And unfortunately, the phone number Malko had found didn't appear in his file.

Tombstone looked up and said:

"I'll try to find out more about Abu Bukatalla from the Cousins."

"Why them?"

"They've got a very good man in Benghazi working for the Arab press. He's undercover; name's Peter Farnborough. He's a Brit, a bit queer, speaks perfect Arabic, and is tight with the Saudi intelligence services. He must know this guy."

"Abu Bukatalla seems like a small-scale *takfiri*," remarked Malko. "Why would he get involved in a complex operation like an attack on a British Airways plane?"

"No idea," admitted Tombstone, "but we've got to find out. You're going to have to find Abu Bukatalla for us."

"How am I going to do that?"

The station chief smiled innocently.

"By going to Benghazi, of course! If you're a bee, you go where the honey is. I realize you may be reluctant to leave your new love, but events have shifted to Libya."

"What can I accomplish there?" protested Malko. "I don't have a contact on the ground, and I don't speak Arabic!"

Tombstone was unruffled.

"We have a nice, comfortable station in Benghazi staffed by some Marines and special-ops guys. They'll give you a vehicle and a fixer. This Peter Farnborough probably knows more than our friends here in Cairo are telling me. The Cousins always tend to be a little secretive."

"How can I even get to Benghazi? There's no transport!"

The American merely smiled.

"Ah, but there's the World Food Program! They have flights from Cairo to Benghazi and Tripoli twice a week. They're normally for members of the various U.N. agencies, but I'm on good terms with the travel manager, Mr. Vayla. I think I can get you a seat on the next flight, which should be Monday."

Malko tried to steer the conversation in another direction.

"Do you have any news of our client? He must have crossed the border by now."

Tombstone shook what remained of his thinning red hair.

"No, he hasn't, and that puzzles me. The Egyptians say he didn't show up at the Sallum crossing, and that's the only one open on the Libyan border."

"Which means he still might be in Egypt," said Malko hopefully.

Libya was receding a bit.

"Anything's possible," agreed the American, "but I don't think so. Why would he ditch his girlfriend and rush off, just to go to Marsa Matruh? The border's completely porous. Go a few miles south, and you'll find dozens of trails that'll get you around the Sallum checkpoint. Al-Senussi has a Libyan network, remember."

A ringing telephone interrupted them. Tombstone listened briefly; then he hung up, looking serious.

"That settles it," he said. "You're going to Libya."

"What happened?"

"Qaddafi was just killed trying to escape from Sirte. Shot in the head by a *thwar* fighter with the Misrata militia. Sirte has fallen, so Libya is free. Now the *real* problems begin. We're facing a major power struggle. The country doesn't have a government, a national army, or any real political structure. And you can count on the Islamists to push it over the edge.

"So we need to support our boy al-Senussi more than ever, and keep him alive. Otherwise, we get an Islamic caliphate and everything that entails. They'll start by cutting thieves' fingers off, and then the whole hand. And if the regime doesn't abandon terrorism, it's going to be Afghanistan in the days of the Taliban all over again. They'll let radical groups come in as 'guests' and look the other way.

"And this will be happening in the shadow of a triple powder keg: Gaza, Egypt, and the AQIM in the south. All those people will come flooding into Libya to get weapons and medical treatment and recruit new followers. Our project *has* to succeed."

Malko was careful not to point out that the idea of reestablishing a king in Libya, even as a constitutional monarch, was more fantasy than reality. The station chief was on a roll and would not be deterred.

"So I'm dropping Cynthia Mulligan," Malko said.

"I know that's hard for your sexual equilibrium," said Tombstone sarcastically, "but maybe you'll find an *Ersatz* in Libya. Isn't that how you say it in your beautiful language?"

"There's more involved than just my sexual appetites," said Malko. "Ibrahim phones Cynthia and gives her news. We'll miss all that. And even assuming he's in Libya, we don't know where. Cynthia's the only person he would tell that to."

This time his argument hit home. Tombstone stood motionless, slowly shaking his head like a wounded elephant.

"Right," he said. "You have a point."

A long silence followed.

"Well, there is one solution," he finally said. "Take her to Libya with you."

Malko almost choked.

"What, in a cage?" he asked. "Just because she's sleeping with me doesn't mean she'll blindly follow me everywhere. I barely know her and she doesn't know the first thing about me."

"Well, the ball's in your court. Treat her to a honeymoon trip."

"In Libya?"

The American made a dismissive gesture.

"Everybody in the Agency says that you're an exceptional seducer, so now you'll get to prove it again. I'll arrange your trip and contact Peter Farnborough. You go persuade the lovely Cynthia."

Sitting in the backseat of the big car that had picked him up in Sallum, al-Senussi fiddled feverishly with his Thuraya. They had crossed the Libyan border on a barely visible trail south of a mountain range. He'd slept in a small house in the middle of the desert and hit the road again at dawn. He was accompanied by two men who said they'd been sent by Abu Bukatalla, and two drivers. They took turns behind the wheel, speeding on a perfectly straight, well-paved road that ran along the coast. They had just passed Tobruk and were stopping to buy gas and water.

Despite al-Senussi's efforts, the Thuraya couldn't get a signal; the satellite phone didn't work from inside a car. Taking advantage of the fact that the drivers and the men accompanying him were having a cup of coffee, he stepped out of the car, shielded the sat phone with his body, and extended its antenna. Moments later, the screen read "Libya."

All he had to do was to key in Cynthia's cell number. It took him three tries for the satellite phone to connect, and when she answered, al-Senussi could have kissed it.

"It's me," he said. "Everything is fine. I'm in Libya."

"Where?"

"I don't know. On the road between Tobruk and Benghazi."

Seeing the drivers returning, he quickly added:

"I'll call you later. I love you."

Cynthia was lounging by the pool when Malko returned from his meeting at the embassy, and she greeted him with a radiant smile. What had happened the night before was clearly a pleasant memory.

Malko sat down on a folding chair next to her.

"Do you have any news of your friend?" he asked.

"Yes. He called me on his satellite phone earlier. He's fine. He's in Libya."

Malko seized the opportunity.

"I think I may have to go there too," he said. "Qaddafi's just been killed, and things are going to start moving."

The young woman put down her magazine.

"What will you be doing there?"

"We've got to get oil production going right away. I told you I was in oil."

The young woman was unmoved.

"And what am I supposed to do?" she asked coolly. "All alone in Cairo."

"Want to come with me?" asked Malko casually.

Cynthia stared at him in astonishment.

"Are you having me on? Libya's a land of savages. Seems there aren't even any more planes."

"If I go there, it'll be on a plane," he said.

"There aren't any planes."

"Not officially, but the United Nations has a few flights. I can get seats on them."

Cynthia gaped at him.

"The United Nations? You know people at the U.N.?"

"My company does, sure."

Malko's proposal clearly repelled her, but she returned to the charge.

"Okay, but what do I do if Ibrahim rings me up? How do I explain that I'm in Libya?"

"He calls you on your cell, so he actually has no way of knowing where you are," Malko pointed out. "And I'd really like it if you came."

The young woman shook her head.

"You're mad! It's impossible. If he ever found out, he'd be furious."

"Are you in love with him?"

Confronted with the direct question, Cynthia was silent for a moment.

"Not really," she admitted in a low voice. "But you've got to do the right thing in life. Besides, we might run into him."

"We won't be staying at a hotel," said Malko. "My company has rented a beautiful villa in Benghazi. You won't have to see anyone."

She was silent for a long time. Finally she said:

"If you swear there's no danger of our bumping into Ibrahim, I'm willing to come."

"That's terrific!" he exclaimed, and kissed her on the neck. "I won't spend all my time working."

"When do we go?"

"I'll let you know. By the way, can I have your cell number?"

"Yes. It's 4477371 4662."

"Okay, I'll call you later and tell you when we're going."

Malko put a piece of paper on Jerry Tombstone's desk.

"This is Cynthia Mulligan's cell phone number," he said. "Al-Senussi called her this morning on his sat phone from somewhere in Libya, so he's definitely there. By accessing her phone, we ought to be able to find out his number. And the next time he calls, it'll be easy to locate him thanks to the Thuraya's built-in GPS. Incidentally, I'll need a second seat on the flight for Benghazi. Cynthia agreed to come with me."

The American was impressed.

"Nice work!" he said. "The seat's no problem; I'll get her added to the list today. And I'll ask our technical division to identify the Thuraya's number. The NATO AWACs screen all communications, so it should be easy, since we know the number being called."

Tombstone suddenly shot Malko a questioning look.

"Are you *sure* she doesn't know about you?"

"I hope not."

"Let's keep our fingers crossed."

"And you'll have to give me some money," said Malko. "Lots of it. Nobody takes credit cards in Libya."

"No problem. We've got everything we need there, including Marine 'babysitters.' They might be useful if we're to protect our man Ibrahim."

Useful indeed, thought Malko, considering the ferocity of the CIA's adversaries. People who didn't hesitate to shoot down a commercial plane with all its passengers just to kill one person had to be treated with respect.

The trip to Libya would be no walk in the park.

CHAPTER 12

Cynthia Mulligan yawned. It was seven o'clock in the morning. Every conversation in the departure lounge of Cairo Airport Terminal 4 was about Muammar Qaddafi's death, which had been announced the day before.

The World Food Program flight would be taking about fifty passengers, mostly journalists or NGO types.

"God, the things you make me do!" she said with a sigh, looking out at the Fokker 100. "That's an awfully small plane. Are you sure it isn't going to crash?"

"One can never be sure of anything," said Malko. "At least we'll die together."

Cynthia wasn't in the mood for humor.

"I don't feel like dying and I don't feel like going to Benghazi," she said. "Besides, we don't know what'll happen in Libya after Qaddafi's death."

"Nothing's going to be happening in Benghazi," he said. "And if you get scared, you can always run to Ibrahim."

She glared at him.

"And tell him what? That I've come to Libya with another man? You want him to cut my throat? You know those Arabs."

The flight was announced, and they walked out onto the tarmac. It was true, the Fokker 100 was indeed quite small. The passengers were an odd menagerie, a mix of NGO staffers who looked like aging students and burly guys with shaved heads who were obviously military.

"We'll be stopping in Marsa Matruh to refuel," the pilot announced. "It will take twenty minutes, but no one must leave the plane."

Cynthia started and leaned over to Malko.

"That sounds frightfully dangerous! What if there's a fire?"

"That's a possibility it's best not to think about," he said soberly.

Privately, Malko exulted. His assignment was turning out better than expected: not only had he had seduced Cynthia, but he'd gotten her to go to Libya with him. Thanks to her, he could pick up al-Senussi's trail there without having to wait for him to call MI6 in Cairo. Which in turn would allow Malko to protect him.

He then had to find Abu Bukatalla, the person most likely behind the British Airways attack, and neutralize him.

That wouldn't be the easiest part of the trip.

The evening before, Tombstone told Malko that the technical division had identified the number of al-Senussi's Thuraya. That meant they could determine his location each time he used the phone. He'd be using it to call Cynthia, of course. The CIA station in Benghazi would meet Malko on arrival and handle logistics for him. His first task would be to contact Peter Farnborough, who might help him find Abu Bukatalla.

Before he left, Tombstone reminded Malko of his assignment's ultimate goal.

"Remember, the point of your trip is to terminate Abu Bukatalla before he kills our boy."

"Al-Senussi may already be dead," said Malko. "We haven't had any news from him since he last called Cynthia."

"I don't think so. Before he left, he saw my opposite number at MI6. He told him that he was going to Libya to contact people like Abu Bukatalla who might support him. I'm sure Abu Bukatalla knows this, and he'll try to use al-Senussi to identify people who would oppose an Islamist takeover of Libya. He wouldn't kill him until after that."

"So why didn't we warn him of the danger he's facing? And what Abu Bukatalla's probably up to?" asked Malko.

"Because I don't want him jumping on the first flight back to London. Al-Senussi's a nice man. He thinks politics is a gentleman's game. I'm hoping that our eliminating Abu Bukatalla will let him carry out his campaign. Anyway, the head of the snake is in Qatar. The emir's the one who wants to establish an Islamic caliphate in Libya."

"But Qatar's an American ally," Malko pointed out. "The biggest naval base in the Gulf is there, and he and Barack Obama are kissing cousins."

"Maybe the emir wipes his mouth afterward," said Tombstone sourly. "Pakistan's a loyal U.S. ally too, but that didn't stop it from letting Osama bin Laden vacation there for a decade, or supporting the Haqqani network, the most virulent of the anti-American Taliban groups.

"Anyway, that's about it. The Benghazi station will give you a Thuraya so you can communicate with me."

Dozing next to Malko, Cynthia was jolted awake when the Fokker landed at Marsa Matruh. She shook him, in a panic.

"I smell petrol! We should get out of here!"

"We're going to Benghazi, not Marsa Matruh," said Malko, summoning the patience of Job.

Fortunately, the refueling was quick, and they had only an hour and a half flight across the desert to Benghazi.

Aside from some rusting Libyan MiGs, an old Airbus, and a pair of Russian Mi-8 helicopters in no condition to fly, the Benghazi airport tarmac lay empty under the broiling sun.

Through the plane window, Malko saw three young men waiting for the flight, chewing gum. They were big guys with square jaws, sunglasses, and loose shirts open over blue jeans. No one would mistake them for NGO personnel.

As Malko stepped off the airstairs, one of them walked over. He was built like a stevedore, with close-cropped hair and an impassive face.

"You Malko?"

"Yes, I am."

"My name's Ted. We came to get you. Follow us."

Cynthia had caught up with Malko and was eyeing the three men curiously.

"They're just here to meet me," he explained. "It's fine."

They walked into the tiny terminal, and Malko pointed out their two suitcases. When Ted bent over to take them off the baggage carousel, they could see the butt of an enormous pistol stuck in his belt.

A brand-new white Cherokee was waiting for them outside. It had tinted windows and no license plates.

Cynthia spoke up.

"I want to have my passport stamped. As a souvenir."

Ted shook his head.

"I'm sorry, miss. There's no customs or immigration here. But we can cobble you a stamp that'll look just as good as a real one, if you like."

They exited under a billboard with the words "Thank You, France" above two Libyan fighters flashing a victory sign. The locals hadn't forgotten that France had been among the rebels' earliest supporters, sending its warplanes on sorties all over the country. In Benghazi, French air attacks had decimated Qaddafi's armored forces.

As they climbed into the back of the Cherokee, Cynthia cried out in pain.

"Ow! I bumped into something on the floor."

She leaned over and picked up an Uzi submachine gun, holding it by the barrel.

Ted turned around.

"I apologize, miss," he said. "That's mine."

He took the weapon and stowed it at his feet. The young woman stared at him, openmouthed.

Beyond the airport, the highway ran straight ahead, lined by dusty eucalyptus trees, with desert on both sides. Not much traffic.

"How are people here reacting to Qaddafi's death?" asked Malko.

"They're firing in the air like crazy," said Ted over his shoulder. "You can tell they're not paying for the ammo."

They entered Benghazi.

Wide, empty avenues in a city as flat as a pancake. Few pedestrians, the occasional local shop, hardly any stoplights, and lots of cars. Endless rows of walls encircling hidden properties alternated with empty lots and little clusters of buildings.

After a half-hour drive, they pulled up in front of a metal gate topped by two ultramodern surveillance cameras and guarded by a Libyan sitting on a folding chair with a Kalashnikov in his lap. Ted honked, and the metal barrier swung open to admit the Cherokee, revealing two men in civvies. Each had an M16 rifle on his shoulder and dark glasses on his head, and carried a pistol and a walkie-talkie.

The Cherokee parked near a beautifully manicured lawn in front of a villa big enough for a pharaoh. Ted led Cynthia and Malko inside.

Deliciously cool thanks to air-conditioning, the place had marble floors, imitation Louis XV gilt furniture, heavy drapes, and carpets. It sure wasn't the Salvation Army.

Ted opened a door to an enormous bedroom, furnished with a twelve-foot bed covered by a quilt woven with gold thread.

"You're in here, sir. There'll be a briefing in the lounge in fifteen minutes."

As he turned to leave, two people came in, a man and a woman. They were barefoot and very slim, with skin that was dark but not black. The woman was quite pretty, with fine features. The man's regular features showed no expression.

Ted turned and came back into the room.

"This is Hissine and Aya. They're from Chad. They'll be taking care of you."

Smiling slightly, the two Chadians bowed and left.

Cynthia flopped onto the bed, looking amazed.

"This place is beautiful!" she exclaimed. "And your company's footing the bill for all this?"

"I think it's renting the house from an expatriate Libyan," said Malko. "If you want to take a bath—"

There was a knock at the door, and the Chadian woman entered, carrying a big basket of fruit. She crouched in front of Cynthia.

"Would you like some fruit, miss?" she asked softly, in English.

The two women's eyes met, and Malko thought he felt a spark fly between them.

When he left the room, Cynthia was peeling an orange.

The meeting was held in a large, ornate lounge with rich carpets, heavy velvet curtains, soft sofas and armchairs, and a long, low table.

A young Libyan man was perched on the edge of a sofa, looking serious and alert. With his short hair, polo shirt, and jeans, he could be mistaken for a student attending a lecture.

"This is Jafar," said Ted. "He'll be your driver and fixer. He's okay. He has a car with Libyan plates and he speaks English."

Jafar smiled and shook Malko's hand.

"I'm a doctor," he said. "Just finished my medical studies. I'm at your disposal."

Ted broke in. "Okay, we'll continue without you."

Jafar slipped out of the room.

The young American proceeded to give Malko the lay of the land.

"This is the Special Operations Group Benghazi station," he

explained. "There are eight of us and we've got six Marines for protection. Our boss is Milton Crawford. He's gone to see what's happening on the Sirte front. We've got secure communications, and thanks to the Chadians, we eat pretty well."

"Does anyone know I'm in Libya?" Malko asked.

"Negative, sir. Nobody keeps tabs on anyone here. We've got all the artillery we need, and I'll show you where to get anything you want. We'll help you any way we can, of course."

"Do you know what I'm here to do?"

Ted gave a predatory smile.

"Sure. To terminate one of those bearded bastards with extreme prejudice. We'll be glad to lend a hand."

Young Ted clearly wasn't exactly a human rights defender. Or at least he drew the line at the white race.

"Excellent," said Malko. "There's a person I have to meet."

"I was briefed on that, sir. A Brit. Here's the number of his cell, but it doesn't work very well. He's staying at the Ouzou Hotel, but I wouldn't see him there, if I were you; you'd be spotted right away. I'd set up a discreet meeting."

He paused.

"That's about it, sir. Jafar's available, and if you need a Marine to go with you anywhere, just say so. Catch you later."

When Malko got back to his room, he found Cynthia in the bath, eating slices of fruit handed to her by the young Chadian woman, who was kneeling on a bath mat next to the tub.

"It's really nice here," said the model with a sigh.

"I've got some work to do," said Malko. "I'll see you in a little while."

Back in the big lounge, he dialed Peter Farnborough's local number.

The Englishman answered right away.

"Jerry gave me your phone number," Malko said. "When can we meet?"

"Tomorrow, if you like. Do you know al-Kish?"

"No."

"It was the Qaddafi troops' old headquarters, out on the Brega highway. Everything's been ransacked or burned and the place is deserted, so it's a nice, quiet place to meet. Shall we say ten o'clock? Do you have transport?"

"Yes, I do."

"All right, then. See you tomorrow."

Very carefully, al-Senussi dialed Cynthia's number. As before, he got no answer, then a busy signal. It was the twentieth time he had tried. Calling with his Thuraya, he should've gotten through. What did this mean?

On arrival in Benghazi he'd been lodged in a little two-story house in the heart of the Old City. His room was on the second floor and had an ancient air conditioner. The ground floor was occupied by several men crowded into a single large room.

He hadn't met with Abu Bukatalla yet, but he didn't care. He'd been able to reach General Abdul Fatah Younes, one of the most powerful men in the new Libya, through his nephew and contact person, Abd al-Raziq.

Younes had been Qaddafi's minister of defense, but he joined the rebellion very early, and the National Transitional Council named him its chief of staff. He was one of the few professionals in the tangled stew of militias, which were headed mostly by amateurs or crackpots. In addition, Younes was an important member of the Obeidi tribe, one of the most powerful in eastern Libya.

If al-Senussi could enlist Younes in his cause, it would attract the other militia chieftains. And he had learned through intermediaries that the general was favorably disposed to his idea of a constitutional monarchy.

Now there was nothing for al-Senussi to do but to wait for Younes to call. The general wasn't in Benghazi, but on the front somewhere to the west.

The Libyan stared at his satellite phone.

If only he were able to reach Cynthia, everything would be perfect.

When Malko returned, Cynthia was stretched out on the bed eating grapes, with her cell phone next to her.

"I tried to call Ibrahim but couldn't get through," she said. "There's no signal. It's strange."

"Wait here. I'll see what's up."

He found Ted in the kitchen making himself scrambled eggs—six of them. The American wasn't surprised by Malko's question.

"That's normal," he said. "Foreign cell phones don't work here. You need either a sat phone or a local SIM card with a lot of credit."

"She needs to contact someone," Malko explained.

"Then she'll have to use your Thuraya," he said, turning back to his eggs.

That wasn't going to work. If Cynthia called her lover on Malko's satellite phone, he would notice and start asking himself questions.

Back in the bedroom, Malko said:

"It's probably a temporary glitch. The NATO AWAC planes sometimes jam communications."

"All right," she said. "Let's go out to dinner. I'd like to see the town."

"We can take a drive around, but the restaurants aren't much good. We'll do better eating here."

Cynthia gave him an odd look.

"Isn't there anyplace to go?"

"Sure, but there aren't many women in public places. This isn't Cairo."

"I'll put on a scarf," she said, sounding half amused, half irritated.

Malko could tell she was nervous and tense.

Just then, someone knocked on the door. It was Ted.

"You better decide about dinner, sir. They aren't very fast."

He was wearing a tank top, and the gun in his belt stood out like a sore thumb. After he left, Cynthia frowned.

"Do your friends carry guns in the house too?" she asked, now frankly suspicious.

"The country's dangerous," said Malko. "Lots of people carry weapons."

Cynthia seemed to think for a moment; then she said flatly:

"Do you think I'm an idiot?"

Malko started. "No, of course not! Why do you say that?"

"There's something weird going on. All your friends have guns, and the place is guarded. It's like a fortress."

"I told you, the country's still at war," Malko insisted. "Qaddafi's only been dead for two days. We have to be careful. Not everyone likes us being here."

Keeping her eyes on his, she spoke again, in the same even tone:

"Ibrahim wrote an important phone number on a piece of paper and left it on the desk in Cairo. Why did you take it?"

CHAPTER 13

Cynthia's level gaze remained on Malko, and it wasn't exactly friendly. She lit a cigarette and continued.

"I think you've been lying to me. You aren't who you claim to be."

"What makes you say that?"

"Everything! All these weapons, this house out in the middle of nowhere, these guys who look like mercenaries. Why did you bring me here?"

"You're the one who wanted to come," he said. "And I'm very happy you did."

"Why did you take that piece of paper? And don't lie."

Her voice was icy.

This was a situation Jerry Tombstone hadn't quite anticipated.

Malko weighed the pros and cons. If he lied to Cynthia now, there was no telling what she might do. It would be hard to keep her from telling her lover the whole story. Malko made up his mind, fast.

"You're right," he said. "I haven't told you the whole truth. I'm not in the oil business."

"So what you do?"

"I work for the American government, and I'm protecting Ibrahim al-Senussi."

"Protecting him? What you mean?"

At this point, Malko figured he might as well tell her everything.

"There are people here in Libya who want to kill him. We're trying to keep that from happening."

"Who is this 'we' you're talking about?"

"A powerful government organization."

"Bullshit!" she snapped, shaking her head. "Nobody's trying to kill Ibrahim. Tell me the real story, or I'll have myself immediately taken back to Cairo."

"That might not be so easy," said Malko incautiously.

Cynthia's look darkened.

"You've kidnapped me! You better watch out. I'm sure there's a British consulate here."

She was becoming dangerous.

"You almost never made it to Cairo," said Malko. "Someone fired a surface-to-air missile at the plane you and Ibrahim were in. Luckily, the guidance system malfunctioned."

"Are you having me on?"

"I'm in no mood for joking."

Enraged, Cynthia jumped to her feet.

"All right, now you're going to tell me why you picked me up. Because you *did* pick me up."

"That's right," he admitted. "I wanted to get close to Ibrahim."

"By sleeping with me? You bastard! You don't give a shit about me!"

Malko tried to calm her down.

"It's true that I was acting under orders, but I can't complain that I got lucky."

Now trembling with rage, she looked him up and down.

"I was a fool for giving in to you."

"I didn't force you," Malko pointed out, smiling apologetically. "You're a very beautiful woman, and sometimes work and pleasure go hand in hand. Besides, I didn't think you would be so easy to seduce."

"So now you're saying I'm a whore!" she snarled. "Okay, that's it! I'm packing my bags."

"And going where, exactly?" he asked sarcastically.

"To Cairo."

"There aren't any trains, buses, or planes. Also, the people here take orders from me."

"And who the hell are you?" she screamed, stamping on the carpet.

"I work for the CIA. In cooperation with your government, as it happens."

"You're a spy?"

"That's a word I don't like. I'm in intelligence, and I'm trying to help Ibrahim play a major political role in the new Libya."

"I know. He wants to be king."

She strode over and stood in front of Malko, her eyes flashing.

"Get the fuck out of my room," she snapped. "I can't stand the sight of you. Tomorrow, we'll see what's what."

Malko left, and the door slammed behind him. Two doors

down the hallway, he found a bedroom almost as big as the first, and moved in. It would be fine for the night, he thought. For the time being, Cynthia wouldn't cause trouble. She couldn't communicate with anybody, and if she tried to walk away, the CIA agents wouldn't let her get far.

Still, he had to resolve the situation. And find out where al-Senussi was.

Cynthia was the only person who could call him. And for her to do that, she had to be on Malko's side.

When al-Senussi hung up the local phone he'd been given, he felt reassured. General Younes's nephew al-Raziq had just called to say that his uncle would be leaving the Sirte front tomorrow and would meet him in Benghazi.

For discretion's sake, Younes wouldn't be accompanied by his usual escort, but only by two trusted colonels. When he reached Benghazi, he would contact the Libyan prince.

Al-Senussi was elated and immediately phoned Abu Bukatalla to share the good news. General Younes was the key element in his plans. Younes knew all the heads of the various militias personally, so he would be able to enlist their support. Younes also hated the Islamists, whom he had pursued for Qaddafi for many years, which is why the Americans trusted him.

A happy al-Senussi tried to reach Cynthia again. But her line was still busy.

Malko was having trouble getting to sleep. He was bothered by his fight with Cynthia, because he absolutely needed her help in order to make contact with al-Senussi.

The huge villa was so quiet you could hear the faint hum of the air-conditioning. So when a sharp cry broke the silence, it was all the more striking.

Heart pounding, Malko leaped out of bed and ran to the hallway. Everything was still. Then a second cry, softer than the first, made him jump. It came from Cynthia's bedroom.

He tiptoed over and listened at the door but heard nothing. Very quietly, he turned the knob. The door wasn't locked, and Malko slipped inside. There was very little light in the room. Holding his breath, he could make out a shape of some sort moving very slightly on the bed. It wasn't until his eyes adjusted to the dark that he could see what it was.

Cynthia was lying on her back, arms outstretched, legs apart. Something dark was moving between her thighs: the head of a woman, who appeared to be pleasuring her.

Malko couldn't be sure, but he had a hunch it was the Chadian maid who had brought Cynthia fruit in the bathroom.

Another brief cry rang out, and Cynthia's legs locked around the head pressed to her crotch.

Malko silently closed the door behind himself and went back to bed. He felt better. Maybe it wasn't *only* because of his lies that Cynthia had thrown him out of their bedroom.

Which augured well for their all-important reconciliation.

Driving the white Cherokee, the CIA stringer named Jafar turned left toward downtown on the avenue known as Carpet Makers Street. In Benghazi, few streets had names. Besides, they all looked alike. They were dead straight, lined with endless walled estates, small clusters of buildings with shops, and plots of vacant land. The city spread in a semicircle around the Old

City port, the lagoon, and the seaside corniche road. The main avenues converging in the center were intersected by five ring roads. The mostly low, dun-colored buildings stood on a flat plain under a harsh, unrelenting sun.

As they drove, Jafar pointed out a building on their left, set back from the street with a huge TV screen planted in a big lawn.

"That's the Venezia," he said. "The food's decent, but there's no alcohol."

About a mile farther, he turned right at one of the few intersections with a stoplight onto an avenue that looked exactly like the last one, then pulled into a big open area surrounded by ruined buildings. The structures no longer had doors or windows and had clearly been sacked and burned.

The place was deserted.

"This is al-Kish," he said. "Qaddafi's troops' old headquarters. When the soldiers took off, people ransacked it."

They seemed to have stolen everything but the paint off the walls.

Malko noticed a shiny new Japanese SUV parked in front of the one of the ruined buildings. He turned to Jafar and asked:

"Does that belong to somebody?"

"No. The Qaddafists left it there on purpose, hoping the *thwars* would take it. It's almost certainly booby-trapped, so no one's touched it."

"And nobody has neutralized it?"

"All the mine-clearing specialists were at the front. Now that Qaddafi's dead, they'll be coming back."

Malko looked around. Where could Peter Farnborough be?

He suddenly noticed a white car off on the right, across from the steel frame of what had once been a warehouse.

Malko walked over to it. The car was a Kia Spectra with Libyan license plates. It was empty. A low whistle made him turn his head. A man wearing a light-colored suit had just appeared behind one of the openings in another ruined building, right across from him.

The man waved, and Malko joined him.

The stranger was short and plump, with a long, sharp nose, white hair, and a brick-red complexion. He looked like an officer in the British Indian Army.

"Peter Farnborough," he said, putting his hand out. "Have any trouble finding the place?"

"No, but it certainly is strange."

"And totally abandoned," said the Brit with a smile. "There's nothing left to loot, so the locals don't come here anymore."

"Where do you live in Benghazi?"

"I'm at the Ouzou Hotel, on the lagoon. Everybody stays there, but there are too many strangers. The NTC doesn't have an intelligence service yet, but all the Islamist groups have spies at the Ouzou." Farnborough laughed. "I'd rather be living in a nice villa, like you."

"Who does my place belong to?"

"To a Libyan who has his fingers in a lot of pies and made a lot of money. He's in Cairo, waiting for things to settle down. Put his villa at the disposal of the U.S. State Department, at least on paper. He pretends not to know it's actually a CIA base."

Farnborough paused.

"So you're looking for Abu Bukatalla, are you?"

"Yes. Do you know him?"

"Met him once. Officially, I'm a correspondent of the Saudi newspaper *Arab News*. I interviewed Abu Bukatalla in Derna, right after he formed his brigade. A tough nut. Refused to go fight on the front because it would mean fighting beside the NATO infidels. He's a fanatical *takfiri*, and the Qatari have loaded him with weapons and money."

"Why do that?"

"Why do you suppose the Pakistanis gave arms and money to the mujahideen in Afghanistan when they were fighting the Russians? Same situation here. Qatar wants to build a real Islamist state, protected from Western influences. Abu Bukatalla is one of their bullyboys."

Farnborough fell silent and glanced around.

"So what can I do for you?" he asked.

"Do you know where Abu Bukatalla is?"

"I used to. He'd set up his headquarters in an old car-body factory in the Abu Ovamina neighborhood next to a public garbage dump. It was convenient for him; he used it to toss out the people he executed—former Qaddafist Mukhabarats who had once pursued the Islamists.

"The day I went to see him, he was interrogating a prisoner, a dark-skinned man on his knees in front of him, wrists bound. Swore he was just a construction laborer; begged not to be killed. Abu Bukatalla told me that he was actually a Nigerian mercenary and had raped Muslim women."

"So what happened?"

"As I was leaving, I heard a burst of AK fire behind me. I turned around and saw the 'mercenary' sprawled on the ground. One of Abu Bukatalla's men had shot him.

"Abu Bukatalla pulled up stakes a few days after this happened, and nobody knows where he is now. Benghazi is full of large, walled properties, and he only has about a hundred men with him, so hiding is easy.

"Still, I have a lead. There's a Spanish woman at the Ouzou

who works with a Danish NGO, teaching people how to clear mines. Her name's Manuela Esteban. She often goes to the arms market in the Assabri neighborhood to buy beer."

"Beer?"

"Yes, they sell beer, too—five dollars a bottle. Manuela was chatting with her supplier and learned that he was in touch with the Abu Bukatalla group, who earn cash by giving him weapons to sell on consignment. I'll go see him and try to find out where Abu Bukatalla is now."

"When do you expect to know?"

"I'll go at the end of the day; the bazaar doesn't open 'til four. You and I could meet again tomorrow, same time."

"Here?"

"No. It's not wise to meet twice at the same place. The best would be to meet at Abu Bukatalla's old headquarters, the body shop. Your driver must know it.

"You leave first," said Farnborough. "I'm going to smoke a cigarette."

After a long handshake, Malko walked back to the Cherokee, passing dozens of graffiti in English and Arabic on the ravaged buildings' walls.

One was quite explicit: "My name is freedom. Next step, Palestine."

Driving out of al-Kish, Jafar hadn't covered more than a hundred yards when a furious burst of gunfire erupted behind them. Heart thudding, Malko swung around to see a pickup racing toward them. The shots were coming from a twin-barrel 23 mm antiaircraft gun mounted in the truck bed, firing like mad.

CHAPTER 14

The pickup truck was gaining on them, and Malko tensely looked for a way they could take evasive action. Jafar wrenched the Cherokee's steering wheel, and they swerved to the side of the road.

"Don't be afraid!" he shouted to Malko.

The pickup pulled level with them, its twin cannons blasting into the sky. It was full of *thwars* with cartridge belts across their chests. Behind the rebels came a dozen cars, one of whose door handles were decorated with lengths of white muslin. From every window of every car, the occupants were firing bursts from AK-47s while yelling slogans punctuated with shouts of "*Allahu akbar!*"

A second pickup brought up the rear, the 14 mm Dushka on its bed firing at an amazing rate. It felt like the siege of Stalingrad.

"It's a wedding!" Jafar shouted over the shooting. "And they're celebrating Qaddafi's death."

The convoy pulled away, and Jafar continued in a normal voice:

"Everybody has an AK-47 now, not like before the revolution. Last year, my younger sister was behaving badly. She was flirting at the university, and my father was afraid that she would have an affair, which would dishonor the family. I bought an AK-47 so I could kill her if she continued. It cost me two thousand dinars. That was very expensive, but it was for the honor of the family. Three months later, after February 17, I could've had one for a hundred dinars."

A violent bump interrupted him. Distracted by his conversation, Jafar hadn't noticed the first of many large speed bumps set in the pavement. They stretched on and on, forcing him to keep his eyes on the road.

Malko was stunned.

"Would you really have killed your sister if she'd had a love affair?"

The young Libyan didn't hesitate.

"Of course! To save the family honor. Normally my father would do it, but he's handicapped."

"Is this a matter of religion?" asked Malko.

"No, it's custom."

"Even if the man agreed to marry her?"

"Too late. The family would already be dishonored. If she had sisters, they could never marry either. Isn't it that way, where you come from?"

"Not really," said Malko.

If America's allies had this kind of attitude, he reflected, what must the Islamists' thinking be like?

Libya was clearly a very different world.

A little farther, they were passed by a pickup truck covered with Arabic writing and carrying a 23 mm gun in the back. It stopped in front of a little house, and a man wearing a T-shirt, bandanna, crossed cartridge belts, and camouflage fatigues got out. He went into the house, leaving the truck parked outside.

"He's a fighter back from the front," Jafar explained.

Malko realized that he'd seen those pickups everywhere, including parked at people's homes like any other car. Civilian vehicles with a gun mount rigged in the truck bed, they were the backbone of the rebel army.

The Cherokee stopped in front of the CIA base. Recognizing the white SUV, the guard spoke into his radio, and the gate swung open a moment later.

Jafar parked between the lawn and the house. Ted came out on the porch and greeted Malko.

"Good trip?"

"Not bad," said Malko. "I'll tell you about it."

They went to sit in the fancy lounge with the gilt furniture. The barefoot Chadian woman with the angelic face brought them coffee.

Malko spoke:

"I'm hoping that I'll find out where Abu Bukatalla is hiding tomorrow. He's the object of an executive order from the president. He's to be sanctioned, and I'll need your help."

"Well, that's good news," Ted said with a grin. "Is he alone?"

"Not exactly. He has about a hundred men."

The American's smile faded.

"There are eight of us, nine counting you," he said. "My guys are good, but I need to bring them back alive! We'll have to find a way to get the bandit off by himself. If there are four or five of them, that's okay too; we can handle that. But otherwise we'd need a Predator, and we don't have any."

Malko hid his disappointment. These special-ops men were cautious killers with their eye on retirement. At the Alamo, they might have tried to negotiate with the Mexicans.

"Okay," he said. "I'll work the problem."

When he stood up, Ted added:

"And we have orders: no collateral damage."

Now Malko had to find a way to make up with Cynthia. He didn't have far to go: the young woman was standing behind the door. Wearing a bath towel and a panicked expression, she gave him a frightened look.

"I heard everything," she blurted. "It's terrible. You're a killer!"

Malko took her by the arm and led her to the bedroom. She slumped onto the bed and lit an American Legend, the only cigarettes to be found in Benghazi. At least her curiosity would spare Malko having to give her a long explanation.

He sat in an armchair facing her and said:

"Okay, you know pretty much everything now. Obviously, when you got together with Ibrahim, you had no way of knowing that he was at the heart of a major political operation. And he didn't tell you, either."

"No, he didn't," she whispered. "He talked about plans, but they seemed kind of amusing."

"I don't want to force you to do things that shock you," Malko continued. "You're free. If you like, I'll ask Ted to have you driven back to Cairo; it's only eight hundred miles. Once there, you'd do well to take the first plane for London and forget all about Ibrahim al-Senussi—and especially everything you've learned here. Otherwise your life will be in danger."

Cynthia Mulligan listened without reacting.

"I don't want to leave," she murmured.

"Why not?"

"I'm afraid."

"So what do you want to do?"

"Stay here," she said, almost inaudibly.

"Why?" he asked in surprise.

"I don't know . . ."

Silence fell, and lasted until Malko spoke again:

"If you stay, you have to be on our side."

"What does that mean?"

"I may have to ask for your help."

"To kill someone?" she asked in horror.

Malko couldn't help but smile.

"No, of course not. I mean, to contact Ibrahim."

"How?"

"I don't know yet. Right now we don't know exactly where in Benghazi he is. Finding out could be vital."

"I can help. I can call him."

"No, not yet. Your cell phones don't work in Libya. The only way to reach him is by calling him on a satellite phone. But for that, his has to be switched on. So for the time being, we can only play a passive role."

"I'm sure he's been trying to get in touch with me."

"That's true, but he can't if he's calling your cell. We have to wait for him to turn on his Thuraya to call MI6 in Cairo or someone else, maybe here in Libya."

"Is he in danger?"

"Yes, but I hope to get him out of danger soon. That's why I'm in Benghazi."

"Was that why you were having that conversation, before?"

"That's right," said Malko without elaborating. "For now, we're standing pat."

If he managed to eliminate Abu Bukatalla, things would be different, and there would be less of a threat to al-Senussi.

"Very well," said Cynthia. "I'm going to get dressed."

The young woman seemed stunned. She was astonished to find herself in a situation and a world whose very existence she hadn't suspected a few days earlier.

Abu Bukatalla was in an outbuilding at his new headquarters, meeting with a brigade man who had just arrived from Benghazi.

Al-Senussi had told Abu Bukatalla that he expected to see General Younes the next day, and asked him to suggest a safe place to meet.

For the *takfiri*, this was a major stroke of luck.

Now that Qaddafi was dead, things were going to start moving on the political level. The National Transitional Council was already powerless against the Misrata militias that had killed the dictator and his son at Sirte. The Misrati were even refusing to hand over the body to the council. NTC members didn't dare travel to Tripoli, which was controlled by Abdelhakim Belhadj.

Qatar had instructed Abu Bukatalla to quickly eliminate any final obstacles to an Islamist takeover. Most of the NTC members had been part of the Qaddafi regime and would soon be out of favor and swept aside. The principal remaining obstacle was Ibrahim al-Senussi.

But before eliminating the pretender to the throne, Abu Bukatalla had some housekeeping to do. To his visitor he said:

"Brother, return to Benghazi and tell our guest that he and I will meet here, after his meeting with General Younes."

It would be the Libyan prince's last meeting.

Sprawled on his bed, al-Senussi lay listening to the sounds of traffic. Here in the Old City, people stayed up very late and businesses were open until midnight. His inability to reach Cynthia was gnawing at him. He didn't know anymore how many times he'd tried calling. Even bare chested, he was drenched with sweat. The old air conditioner produced more noise than cold air.

He was counting the hours until his meeting with Younes, his main reason for coming to Benghazi. Once he convinced General Younes to support him, he was definitely heading back to Cairo. He would return to Libya only in response to a call by the people, prompted by his new friends. And this time, he would go with Cynthia.

Suddenly, he couldn't stand it anymore. He had to talk to her. He took his Thuraya and went up onto the terrace. Thanks to a breeze from the sea, it was a little cooler there. The sky glittered with stars, and a nearby mosque sounded a piercing cry, calling the faithful to prayer.

Al-Senussi pulled out the Thuraya's antenna, and it quickly locked onto the satellite stationed above the Indian Ocean. The moment the screen read "Libya," he dialed the Four Seasons, whose number was in his cell's memory. The number rang for a few seconds, and a voice in Arabic answered with the name of the Cairo hotel.

"Suite 2704, please," said al-Senussi in Arabic.

After a few moments of silence, the operator said, "No answer, sir. The suite is unoccupied."

"Are you sure?" al-Senussi insisted.

"Quite sure, sir. The suite has been free for the last three days. Would you like to speak to the front desk?"

"Yes, please."

He soon had a desk clerk on the line, who confirmed that the suite had been empty for three days. Also, that the bill had been paid.

"By the woman?"

The clerk didn't know.

Al-Senussi didn't press the point. He knew the main thing, which was that Cynthia was no longer at the hotel. Now furious, he tried her cell phone for the hundredth time.

Without result.

If she'd gone back to England, she could at least have left him a message.

Where was she?

When al-Senussi went back downstairs, he still didn't have an answer to the question. Feeling angry and depressed, he flopped down on the bed. He didn't even have a beer to cheer him up.

"I just talked to the Cairo station," said Ted. "You're to call Mr. Tombstone—it's urgent."

Cynthia was in the bathroom, getting ready. Malko took his Thuraya and went out on the lawn. Night was falling. Two minutes later, he had Jerry Tombstone on the line.

"Bingo!" crowed the American. "NATO says al-Senussi just used his Thuraya. Thanks to the built-in GPS, we've been able to locate his position by matching his coordinates on a map of Benghazi. The call was made from a location in the Old City, at the corner of al-Sharif and Masawi Streets. The Thuraya doesn't broadcast a signal from inside a house, so he either called from the street or from a rooftop. Try to locate him first thing in the morning."

"We'll take care of it," Malko promised.

"There's one more thing," added the station chief. "Al-Senussi phoned the Four Seasons, so he now knows that Mulligan isn't there. You'll have to handle that."

"I'll do what I can."

"How's your search for Abu Bukatalla coming? Now that Qaddafi's dead, things are starting to move."

"Our Six contact is supposed to tell me his hiding place tomorrow," said Malko. "But there's a problem: our friends here aren't all that eager. There aren't enough of them for serious action."

"If need be, we'll pick up al-Senussi and get him to safety. Mulligan might be helpful there."

Malko went into the house, to the bedroom. Cynthia was coming out of the bathroom in a cloud of perfume. She wore makeup, an attractive shade of lipstick, and a form-hugging cotton dress that buttoned down the front.

She seemed quite recovered from the morning's drama.

"Are you feeling better?" asked Malko.

The young woman smiled, a new gleam in her gray eyes.

"Yes. When I heard you talking about killing someone, I had feelings I've never experienced before. It was like being in the movies. It was intense."

Malko grinned. "We operate in a world where we run on adrenaline and do things ordinary people can't. In any case, you're looking very beautiful this evening."

"Thanks. Where are you taking me to dinner?"

She must have thought she was in Cairo.

"That's a bit of a problem," said Malko with a smile. "First, because the few restaurants around here are terrible, and second, because this isn't a good time to show ourselves in public. But I'll ask Ted if we can go out."

The special-ops leader was nonplussed, but had a suggestion.

"If the young lady wants to eat a halfway decent meal, we could go to the Bala Beach. It's on the coast road and the fish is fresh; we eat there from time to time. Of course, they only have nonalcoholic beer."

"Going out doesn't seem very wise," Malko objected.

"It'll be okay. We have an old Ford Winner with local plates. It's discreet. And we can follow in a Cherokee."

He paused.

"Just one thing: the young lady has to change her clothes. Otherwise, people will notice her."

Suddenly Malko had an idea.

"We could drive there by way of the Old City, couldn't we? I'd like to check out the place where al-Senussi is. I have the address."

"Show me," said Ted.

While Cynthia was changing, they sat down in the kitchen. The American unfolded a map of Benghazi that was more detailed than Malko's, and quickly found the location the Thuraya signal came from.

"We could swing by there," said Ted. "I'll drive in front. When we get to the intersection of al-Sharif and Masawi, I'll tap my brakes, and you'll see my taillights come on. We won't stop, of course."

"Perfect!" said Malko.

He went to fetch Cynthia. Wearing jeans, a head scarf, and a modest blouse with a high collar, she was almost decent. Though when she walked, she swung her hips in a way unknown in the Quran.

They joined Ted, who was waiting by the lawn with three Marines.

"I'll drive lead, and you'll follow, with Bill driving," he said. "There'll be four of us in the Cherokee. Two will stay with the car and two will eat in the restaurant. Foreigners often go there."

Malko's car was an old blue Ford that smelled bad. Cynthia got into the back and a young Marine took the wheel. Malko sat in the passenger seat.

The gate slowly swung open and they drove out onto the unpaved road.

There was no one in sight.

By night, Benghazi with its lights had a certain charm. It took them a half hour to reach first the lagoon, then the Old City. Its streets were full of people. There were many women in *niqab* or veiled; not a single head was uncovered. There were dozens of shoe stores on 2A Street, the main business drag; with so many shoes, you would think the Libyans were millipedes.

Malko kept his eye on the Cherokee twenty yards ahead of them. Suddenly it slowed, and its taillights flashed just before an intersection. It was the place where al-Senussi was located. Beyond the intersection on the left was an old one-story house, with a pickup truck with a machine gun parked out front. Malko looked up. There were no lights in the windows, but the house had a terrace roof. It looked like every other house around.

They drove to the coast and turned right on Ahmed Rafiq al-Mahdawi, leaving al-Tahrir Square to their left. There were cars parked here and there, but not many pedestrians. The Cherokee passed a restaurant built above the highway, then pulled over and stopped.

The Bala Beach dining room was completely empty. In a small side room, fresh fish were laid out on a bed of ice.

Two of the CIA men walked back from the Cherokee to the restaurant. The SUV then made a U-turn, parked on a sandy pullout on the other side of the highway where it had a clear view in both directions, and switched off its lights.

Cynthia and Malko climbed the steps to the restaurant and were greeted by the owner, who showed them the fish.

"Lobster!" he cried, waving a boiled spiny lobster under Malko's nose.

He took the crustacean and examined it. It had been cooked a long time before and its claws were slightly greenish. To be on the safe side, he chose a large dorado instead.

There were just the four of them in the restaurant, and the two operatives were pretending not to know each other. But Cynthia seemed delighted.

"It's pretty here," she said. "And the air's nice."

It was true; a warm breeze was blowing in from the sea. She and Malko drank mineral water while the dorado was being cooked. As they waited, an old violinist popped up at the end of the room, as if he'd been stored in a closet somewhere. To their surprise, he went to stand behind the cash register and began to play.

The violinist disappeared unbidden when the dorado came out, surrounded by gritty-looking vegetables.

All in all, it wasn't half bad.

Malko leaned over to Cynthia and said, "Earlier, we passed the place where your friend Ibrahim is staying."

He explained the operation.

"I hope he didn't see me!" she said in alarm.

The two Americans went out just before Malko and Cynthia did. There were only a few shops still open on the long corniche road. The drive home was uneventful, with almost no traffic.

The moment they were in the bedroom, Cynthia turned to Malko.

"Thank you," she said.

Moments later, she was pressing first her lips, then her whole body against him. She reached down to draw his stiffening penis from his alpaca trousers.

Malko had never seen her like this.

She tore off her blouse, then shoved her jeans down. She walked over and let herself fall back on the bed. She spread her legs apart, then lifted herself to slip off the scrap of black lace that covered so little of her belly.

Ever the gentleman, and knowing Cynthia's preferences, Malko moved his head toward her exposed crotch, but she grabbed him by the hair.

"No," she said. "Not tonight."

She hadn't even taken off her bra, and Malko was already as

hard as iron. Cynthia gave a little flick of her hips, as if to ease him into her, then gave a sigh of delight.

"Fuck me."

He lifted and bent her legs back and proceeded to pound at her with powerful thrusts of his hips.

Gripping his back, Cynthia started to scream. She was coming and coming.

When she felt Malko was about to explode, she shouted:

"You're so big! Harder, darling, harder!"

Malko collapsed on her with a hoarse shout. This was a long way from their first sexual encounter. When he started to pull out, Cynthia held on to him.

"Stay there," she said. "I want you to fuck me again."

This was a switch from her usual program. As if she could tell what he was thinking, she said:

"I feel as if I'm becoming a different woman. I always used to find men so brutal. But everything that's happened in the last few days has shaken me up. And I've never met a man like you. My boyfriends were pussycats, sometimes bisexual, too. Like companion animals."

"What about Ibrahim?"

"No, not him. He pursued me so desperately, I found it touching. But he just wanted to get off with me. He didn't care if I enjoyed it or not."

"But I didn't do anything special," said Malko. "And I was rough, too."

Cynthia gave a throaty laugh.

"Maybe I'm being unfair! Or else I've fallen in love with another world."

She very slowly began to move her hips until she could feel Malko getting hard deep inside her. He made love to her again, more gently, and she began to moan quietly. Cynthia really did like gentleness.

Later, sexually spent, Malko found himself thinking that if Peter Farnborough led him to Abu Bukatalla tomorrow, it would really be a red-letter day.

CHAPTER 15

For the last half hour, the two Cherokees had been criss-crossing the Assilmani neighborhood inside the al-Jala Hospital Ring Road. Ted asked several pedestrians where Abu Bukatalla's old headquarters was located, but nobody would tell him.

Finally, he stopped at an Al-Rahla gas station—the brand with the handsome camel on its logo—on the Shola Square roundabout. The owner knew where the headquarters was, but his directions were so complicated that Ted handed him a fifty-dinar bill and said, "Give us a guide."

Pressed into service, one of the attendants climbed into the Cherokee. Malko went to sit in back between two Kevlar-clad special-ops men. M16s and ammo magazines littered the floor.

After they'd driven for another ten minutes, the gas jockey pointed to the entrance of a complex below Maryif Road: a group of apparently abandoned buildings next to a huge mound of garbage. The Cherokee stopped in the middle of a courtyard surrounded by empty buildings. The other SUV stayed near the entrance, to deal with any unexpected company.

Debris lay everywhere, including several wrecked cars. The moment they got out, their guide took off running, without giving them time to ask him a single question.

Escorted by two Marines, Malko walked around the buildings. Given their size, they must have been barracks.

There was no one around.

He looked at his watch. Peter Farnborough should have been there half an hour ago.

Malko was getting a bad feeling. He dialed the MI6 agent's cell phone but immediately got his voice mail.

They walked around the area for another ten minutes, with Ted increasingly on edge.

"This is a trap," he muttered. "We should get out of here."

"We can't," said Malko. "It's too important. Let's go talk to the guys working at the dump."

Ted led their group over to the big public garbage dump on their right. The workers there looked very surprised to see them. There weren't many foreigners in Benghazi, and certainly none at the dump. The stench was awful.

Ted asked some questions in Arabic, then turned to Malko.

"They say this was Abu Bukatalla's headquarters, but he left more than a month ago."

That much Malko already knew.

"Ask them if they saw anybody today. Tell them we were supposed to meet a foreigner here."

The man shook his head, then said:

"Someone came about an hour ago. Two guys in a pickup who tossed out a big bag. One of them said that if I saw any foreigners I should give it to them."

Malko felt the blood draining from his face.

"Where's the bag?"

"Over there, in the dump truck or next to it," said the man. "That's the garbage we're about to burn."

"Can you dig it out?"

The man hesitated, and a twenty-dinar bill changed hands. The group walked deeper into the dump, and the stench got even worse. Ted was holding his nose with his left hand. Their man shouted to some workers who were loading a dump truck. Reluctantly, they climbed into the truck and started rummaging around. A few minutes later, they pulled out a bag and lay it on a pile of garbage.

Malko was about to rush over, but Ted stopped him.

"Watch out! It might be booby-trapped."

The American kneeled next to the bag and examined it. He could see that it was closed with an ordinary string. He tugged on the string, then cut it. Very carefully, he opened the bag.

Seeing him jump backward, Malko expected to hear an explosion, but nothing happened.

Looking thunderstruck, Ted waved Malko over. He was as pale as a ghost.

"Take a look," he said in a choked voice.

Malko opened the bag a bit and saw what he first thought was a furry animal. Looking more closely, he realized it was white hair on a scalp.

Mastering his disgust, he opened the bag wider, this time revealing a human head.

The dead man's eyes had been gouged out, and their sockets were crusted with blood. His hands were tied behind his back. Despite this butchery, Malko had no trouble recognizing him. It was Peter Farnborough.

The body lay on a pile of garbage in the middle of the dump. Farnborough was wearing the same clothes he'd had on at their first meeting. Carefully turning the body, they found a bloody hole in his neck. He had been shot execution style. There was no way to know if they'd gouged his eyes out before or afterward.

Ted slowly made the sign of the cross.

"Goddamn the bastards who did this," he said dully.

The worker said something in Arabic, and Ted glared at him, looking ready to strangle the man.

"He wants to know if they should put the body back in the dump truck."

"Tell him that we aren't Muslims, but we respect the dead," said Malko. "Ask him who brought this body."

Ted translated the answer.

"*Thwars*, he says. They had AK-47s and seemed to know what they were doing."

"What *thwars*?" Malko insisted.

The dump worker clearly didn't understand what he meant. Malko asked the question differently.

"Did they have beards?"

"Of course. They looked like good Muslims."

So they were probably Islamists.

"Why didn't you tell the police?"

The worker shrugged.

"We find bodies all the time," he said. "They're traitors. Besides, there's no more police."

"But that man was a foreigner."

"There are also foreign mercenaries," he said.

Anxious to get back to work, the man turned away and resumed loading the truck.

Two of the agents brought a big green tarp and wrapped the MI6 agent's body in it.

They left Abu Bukatalla's old headquarters a few minutes later, driving in silence. Malko realized that his lead to the *takfiri* had been cut. He would have to move Ibrahim al-Senussi to safety as soon as possible.

When Ted slowed to turn onto the dirt road leading to their base, Malko saw him notice something in his rearview mirror.

"A green car just drove by," said the American. "I saw it earlier, when we were leaving the dump."

So they may have been followed.

Malko got out first. He had to talk to Jerry Tombstone immediately. Exfiltrating Ibrahim al-Senussi wasn't going to be easy, even assuming he was still in the same location.

Abu Bukatalla listened as the militiaman he'd sent to watch the dump reported.

It was very edifying.

The description of one of the foreigners matched that of the CIA agent in Cairo who knew al-Senussi's girlfriend. So the man was now active here in Benghazi. If it hadn't been for the alertness of one of Abu Bukatalla's partners, he might have had a CIA commando bursting into his new headquarters.

Right when he was in the final phase of his operation.

He needed at least forty-eight hours to wrap everything up and kill the pretender to the country's throne. He would then have completed the mission Qatar had assigned him.

And earned an important position in the new Libya.

He now had to quickly dispatch the CIA agent, who was getting too close for comfort. It wasn't clear how to accomplish that, however. Even he couldn't afford to openly attack the Americans, who were the NTC's allies. He would have to set a trap.

Standing out on the lawn, Malko had just told Tombstone about Peter Farnborough's brutal murder. The Cairo CIA station chief's reaction was equally brutal.

"We've got to kill this Abu Bukatalla guy, and right away. Do you have any other leads to him?"

"I have a name," said Malko. "A Spanish woman named Manuela Esteban who works for an NGO. She might know who set Farnborough up. She's staying at the Ouzou Hotel, but that's all I know."

"Follow that lead," said Tombstone. "I'll give Herb Mallows the bad news about what happened to Farnborough. He's the Cousins' representative here."

"Okay," said Malko. "I'll go to the Ouzou and try to find the woman."

When he went inside, Cynthia was emerging from her bedroom.

"What are we doing today?" she asked. "I'd like to see the city in daylight."

Malko hadn't told her about Farnborough's death. She'd been asleep when he left for their meeting.

"I do have to go into town," he said. "You can come along, but you'll have to stay in the car."

They left the base a few minutes later, with Ted at the wheel and a Marine in the back next to Cynthia. Malko wanted to take advantage of the trip to the Ouzou to check out the place where al-Senussi was supposed to be. On their way to the hotel they crossed the Old City and reached al-Tahrir Square, where the Revolution was celebrated every Friday.

By daylight, the house pinpointed by al-Senussi's GPS was an old yellowish place with a flat roof. Its doors and windows were all closed, and the armed pickup was still parked in front.

They drove along the harbor, passing a T-72 tank with its barrel pointed out to sea. The wall opposite was plastered with photographs of martyrs.

A little farther on, the plaza was covered by black canvas with white stripes designed to help the faithful line up facing Mecca for Friday prayers. From a distance, the stripes made it look like a competition swimming pool.

Facing the square was another huge billboard reading "Thank You, France" in French and Arabic, with a picture of Nicholas Sarkozy. Unfortunately, the flag topping this expression of gratitude was that of Slovakia.

Cynthia seemed impressed by what she saw.

"Is it true that Qaddafi nearly destroyed the city?" she asked.

"Yes, and he would have succeeded if NATO hadn't taken action."

They drove around the lagoon—23rd July Lake—on Algeria Street to the Ouzou. Ted took the turnoff to the hotel, which was set back from the street and guarded by a checkpoint manned by *thwars* under a big umbrella with the black, green, and red Libyan flag.

To deter car bombs, vehicles were first given a cursory inspection, then shunted off to a parking garage.

Malko left Cynthia and the Americans in the garage and went into the hotel.

He very much hoped he could find Manuela Esteban.

The alarm on the metal detector at the lobby entrance beeped continuously under the indifferent gaze of the rebels manning it. It was more symbolic than anything else. The Ouzou housed most of the journalists in Benghazi, and their gear was constantly setting off the alarm, coming and going.

Malko walked over to the front desk, where the smiling Libyan clerk spoke only Arabic and had no idea what Malko wanted. He realized that the name Manuela Esteban alone wouldn't be enough to find Farnborough's friend.

A dozen hotel guests, men mostly, were sitting in the lobby's leather armchairs, so Malko started making the rounds.

At the fourth chair, he found what he was looking for: a reporter who knew Esteban.

"She went to Ra's Lanuf for two days, to teach mine-clearing classes," the man said. "Otherwise, she's in Room 315. She's very short. You can't miss her."

Malko thanked him and left the hotel. He would just have to be patient.

"We're going home," he told Ted when he reached the Cherokee.

Leaving the hotel, they took Urubah Road south toward the First Ring Road.

Before they'd gone a hundred yards, Ted announced calmly:

"We're being followed, sir. An armed pickup is trying to catch up with us."

Malko turned around and saw a twin-barreled gun mount in the pickup's bed. The guns weren't firing, but for some reason, he felt threatened. There were several men inside and in the back of the truck.

Ted accelerated.

Two hundred yards farther, they reached the junction with the First Ring Road. Seeing a second armed pickup parked by the side of the road, Ted cursed. The moment it spotted the Cherokee, it pulled out and stopped, blocking the roadway. Malko could see its cannons swinging around to bear. The moment they passed in front of them, the guns would riddle their vehicle.

"Shit, shit, shit!" Ted swore.

Instead of turning, he continued south on Urubah Road.

The first pickup was still behind them, apparently holding its fire until they were in an area without any houses. The Marine in the backseat was feverishly talking into his radio.

"We've got to lose them!" said Malko.

They had to be Abu Bukatalla's men and had probably been following them ever since they left the base. The Cherokee sped up and gained some ground on the pickup. They were racing due south and soon found themselves in open desert, between stretches of unfinished buildings.

"We're on the Brega highway," Ted announced.

The pickup truck was still behind them but wasn't gaining.

"What happened here?" asked Cynthia, pointing to a gutted troop transport lying by the right side of the road. It had been hit by a missile.

"NATO planes," said Ted tersely. "Nice work."

A mile farther, a T-72 tank, its treads blown off, was permanently parked under a tree. Both sides of the highway along here were littered with the hulks of tanks and armored vehicles, their turrets and treads destroyed and their flanks pierced.

There couldn't have been many survivors. This was the road on which NATO planes had destroyed the armored column that Qaddafi sent to attack Benghazi in February. On such completely flat terrain, without so much as a cactus, even a novice pilot could hit a tank with an air-to-ground missile.

Particularly since the armored vehicles had no antiaircraft defense.

The rusting metal carcasses, emblazoned with vengeful slogans, stretched for a dozen miles. If the armored column had reached Benghazi, it would have made quick work of the pickup trucks with their machine guns and light cannons.

In front of the Cherokee, the road toward Ajdabiya and Ra's Lanuf ran south to the horizon.

Malko turned around. The pickup was still on their tail.

"Where are we going?" asked Cynthia, who hadn't noticed anything amiss.

Malko didn't have time to answer her. He had just seen orange flames spitting from the pickup's twin cannons. Now that there weren't any more houses nearby, it was attacking.

A dull thud shook the Cherokee. A shell had knocked something from the back of the SUV. Other shells ricocheted off the pavement, kicking up chunks of asphalt.

Cynthia screamed, and Ted accelerated even more. They were driving faster than the pickup, but nothing can outrun a 23 mm shell. Malko looked around: nothing but desert as far as the eye could see. They had about as much chance of escaping the pickup's weapons as Qaddafi's armored vehicles had of escaping the NATO fighter planes.

"They're shooting at us!" Cynthia screamed.

Luckily, the rebel pickup was being jolted by the highway's many potholes and had trouble taking aim. But if just one shell hit the Cherokee squarely, they would all be dead.

Frowning, Ted turned to Malko. In a level voice, he said, "We're running out of gas, sir."

CHAPTER 16

A fresh volley of cannon fire sent chunks of pavement skittering left of the Cherokee, and Ted involuntarily swerved.

Cynthia screamed again.

Malko's mind was racing, but it wasn't producing any solutions. Death was very close now. If their Cherokee ran out of gas, it would be a sitting duck. Even if it didn't, the 23 mm shells would get them sooner or later.

Ted had the pedal to the floor, but they still weren't moving fast enough to get out of range.

Suddenly Malko noticed a group of rusting armored vehicles on the stony desert off to the right, including a big self-propelled howitzer. Its tank tracks had been blown off, and its impressive 155 mm cannon would never fire again. But the howitzer itself wasn't damaged; it had just lost its tracks and later been looted. Its armored sides were covered with inscriptions in Arabic.

The sight of a square hatch on the turret gave Malko an idea. He turned to Ted and yelled, "Head for that howitzer over on the right."

A dirt road ran perpendicular to the highway, and the special-ops leader swerved onto it, then raced toward the howitzer. He drove around behind it and stopped. The rebels' pickup truck was still on the highway, but was sure to follow.

Malko got out, leading Cynthia by the hand. Ted and the Marine jumped out, Uzis at the ready. The howitzer's bulk shielded them from fire from the pickup.

Malko pushed the young woman toward the square hatch.

"Quick, get inside!"

He helped her climb the side of the howitzer, and she crawled through the hatch. Malko shoved her down inside, then followed. The stench in the crew quarters was nauseating. At almost the same moment they heard the boom-boom-boom of the 23 mm cannons, they felt the shells' impact on the tank's heavy armor.

The two Americans dove in headfirst. There was nothing left of the howitzer but the steel walls and the cannon's breech. Everything else had been stripped.

Ted handed Malko an Uzi with a magazine in place.

"You take care of those tangos!" he shouted. "I'll call the cavalry."

A volley of detonations could be heard outside. The pickup had taken up position on the dirt road and was firing at them steadily.

But the 23 mm shells were completely ineffective against the howitzer's armor. They crumpled against the steel plate or ricocheted off it like tennis balls. Malko stood by one of the hatches, observing the pickup. Its driver realized his guns were having no effect on the enormous howitzer, so he pulled forward to better aim at the hatches.

Malko waited, then fired a short burst with the Uzi, hitting the front of the pickup. It quickly backed away, then resumed its pointless firing.

Ted had been yelling into his radio. When he hung up, he said to Malko, "They're coming with an RPG. Gonna blow those bastards away!"

"How long will it take them?"

"Quarter of an hour, at least."

A long time.

Malko risked a look outside and saw several men with AK-47s jump from the pickup and advance toward the motionless howitzer.

He waited until the rebels had covered half the distance before opening fire. One man fell and the others precipitously retreated. Out in the open without any cover, they were particularly vulnerable. Ted joined in, firing several short bursts with a second Uzi.

Another *thwar* fell.

The others came back and dragged their wounded to the pickup. The man operating the twin-barreled gun continued to waste ammo plinking at the howitzer.

The men in the pickup clearly hadn't expected this tactic.

Suddenly Ted gave a happy yell:

"They're pulling out!"

It was true. As soon as the two wounded rebels were loaded onto the pickup's bed, it drove away.

Malko looked at his watch. Less than five minutes had passed since they took shelter in the armored vehicle.

At the bottom of the compartment, Cynthia sat huddled against the steel wall, sobbing convulsively.

Malko knelt down next to her.

"Everything's going to be okay," he said quietly.

The pickup truck was now out of sight, but it could be stopped farther down the road, lying in wait.

Ted got back on the radio to guide his men. A civilian car passed on the dirt road, apparently without noticing anything amiss. About ten minutes later, two white Cherokees appeared on the Brega highway. They skidded onto the dirt road like Le Mans racers and slammed to a stop next to the howitzer's barrel.

Seven men burst from the vehicles wearing helmets and bulletproof vests and carrying M16s with grenade launchers. The last man out carried a loaded RPG-7 and a canvas backpack with three spare grenades.

Ted, Malko, and the Marine climbed out of the howitzer, glad to be breathing fresh air after the stench inside.

"Where are the bandits?" asked the man with the RPG.

"Didn't you see them on the highway?"

"No. They must have turned off somewhere."

"Okay, let's move out," said Ted. "You lead, we'll follow, and Max is the drag."

That's when Malko noticed the big American flags mounted on poles on the backs of the two vehicles.

"It's good insurance," Ted said with a grin. "If somebody shoots at us, it's an act of war, 'cause we're NTC allies. I call in a NATO air strike and pulverize them."

Very effective.

They were getting into their vehicles when Malko suddenly yelped, "Cynthia!"

He'd forgotten she was still inside the howitzer.

He went over and stuck his head down the hatch.

"Cynthia?"

She didn't answer right away. Then she said, "What's going on? I'm scared."

"They're gone," Malko assured her.

She eventually began to move, and he was able to take her hand and haul her out. She was absolutely terrified, shaking all over. She let him push her into the Cherokee, and she collapsed on the seat looking haggard and in shock.

The little convoy started up, flags flying.

A few miles down the road they saw a checkpoint on the right that they hadn't noticed before. The rebels manning it waved at them joyously. In his enthusiasm, one fired an AK volley into the air.

Cynthia screamed and grabbed for Malko.

"They're not shooting at us," he said reassuringly.

They continued driving at top speed, with people often waving as they passed, applauding the American flag.

Benghazi was a friendly city—it just wasn't all that safe.

They pulled into the CIA base a half hour later. Cynthia was dead on her feet and had to be helped out of the car. When Malko got her to their room, she collapsed on the bed. The Chadian woman named Aya heard the noise and silently appeared.

"She's in shock," Malko told her. "Run her a bath, then try to find her a sleeping pill."

He grabbed his Thuraya and ran out onto the lawn. He absolutely had to talk to Jerry Tombstone and coordinate what to do next.

"We've got to extract Ibrahim as fast as possible," the CIA chief said decisively. "We don't know how soon we'll be able to get to Abu Bukatalla."

"How do we do it?" asked Malko.

There was a silence on the line, then Tombstone said, "We absolutely have to contact him. Here's his sat phone number: +8787 72394053. Call him. Better yet, have Cynthia Mulligan call him."

"What if the Thuraya isn't turned on?"

"It has voice mail. She can leave a message to call her back on your Thuraya."

"He'll be furious when he calls back," remarked Malko. "He thinks she's still in Cairo, somewhere."

"That's just too bad. It's the only sure way of reaching him. Anyway, Ibrahim will be so happy to hear his sweetheart's voice, he'll swallow her lies."

"There are an awful lot of them."

"She can make up some sort of fairy tale. The main thing is to get him out of where he is and move him to safety."

"Here?"

"Maybe. I'll ask Langley for instructions."

"Fine, I'll start the ball rolling. I just hope Ibrahim doesn't blow up in our faces."

"It shouldn't keep you from continuing to track Abu Bukatalla," said Tombstone.

"There's nothing I can do until Manuela Esteban gets back."

Their conversation over, Malko went to the bedroom. Aya was tucking an unconscious Cynthia under the covers.

"She didn't take a bath," said the Chadian. "Too tired. I gave her a sleeping pill."

Malko leaned over the young woman and tried to wake her, in vain. No response. Between the sleeping pill and her fright, Cynthia was out of commission for the time being. She would have to be conscious before she could call her lover.

Standing behind the shutters, Ibrahim al-Senussi cocked an ear every time he heard traffic on al-Sharif Street. Whenever a car braked, his heart began to pound. But the cars never stopped. They just slowed, went through the intersection, and drove on.

General Younes should have arrived more than an hour ago, as he'd promised on the phone. Al-Senussi had called the general's cell a dozen times, but it went immediately to voice mail. Feeling increasingly concerned, he went downstairs to consult the two militiamen guarding the house, but they didn't know anything.

Something had happened.

Now al-Senussi was pacing, feeling more and more worried. The meeting with Younes was the whole point of his trip to Libya.

He tried to call Abu Bukatalla, but without success.

To make things worse, his air conditioner had broken down, and the heat in the little room was unbearable.

If General Younes wasn't there by morning, he decided, he would call the MI6 agent in Benghazi. His name was Peter, and Ibrahim had his phone number.

General Abdul Fatah Younes was dozing, supported by his seat belt, his head on the headrest. Since Ra's Lanuf, they had driven more than two hundred miles on a boringly straight road.

Next to him, his driver was having trouble keeping his eyes open. In the back, the two colonels accompanying the general were sound asleep.

The NTC chief of staff normally traveled with a more impressive escort: a dozen heavily armed pickups driven by men whose loyalty he could rely on. But for this meeting with

King Idris's grandson, Younes had opted for discretion. As soon as he picked Ibrahim al-Senussi up, he would take him to one of his tribe's properties outside Benghazi. It would be a safe place for them to hold their discussions.

Younes was wearing a camouflage uniform with his service medals and the red collar insignia indicating his rank. An impressive-looking man, he had an energetic face, a strong nose, and a shock of gray hair.

The car suddenly slowed, and Younes opened his eyes. There were lights on the road up ahead, though they hadn't yet reached downtown Benghazi. He could make out an armored vehicle positioned across the highway, its barrel pointed in his direction. There was no way around it.

His driver stopped, and the two colonels woke up.

The car was immediately surrounded by armed men wearing full beards and ragtag outfits.

The driver rolled down his window.

"Let us through," he said angrily. "This is General Abdul Younes."

"We know that," the nearest bearded man said smoothly. He put his hand on his heart. "Salaam alaikum! The NTC sent us to escort the general. You'll be driving with us."

Younes was surprised.

"Who sent you?" he asked.

"The leader of the February 17 Brigade," said the man, and walked away.

The armored vehicle pulled back, and they drove on, now boxed in by a dozen pickups full of rebels ahead and behind.

Puzzled and concerned, Younes took out his cell and called NTC president Mustafa Abdel-Jalil's deputy on his direct line.

The man said he had absolutely no idea what Younes was talking about. But that didn't mean much, given the council's usual disarray. He promised to check and call the general back.

Younes hung up. His men were nearly two hundred miles away, in the south. It would take more than the two colonels, who were now wide awake, to protect him.

Tensely, he looked out the window. Despite the darkness, he knew exactly where he was, recognizing a ruined building that stood at the junction with the Fifth Ring Road. But the convoy turned right, heading east. This absolutely wasn't the direction of downtown, which was to the north.

Now Younes was sure something was wrong. He picked up his folding Kalashnikov from the floor of the car, prepared to fight for his life.

The long convoy was passing vacant lots in a deserted neighborhood.

Where were they going?

He phoned the NTC again but got no answer.

Now on edge, he continued to look out the window and chambered a round in his assault rifle.

Cynthia was still deeply asleep. Malko realized he couldn't count on her until morning.

There was no point in alerting Tombstone about the delay. Nothing serious was likely to happen between now and daybreak, and the base's guard had been reinforced in case their adversaries decided to launch an attack.

Malko walked out onto the lawn and contemplated the

starry sky. As usual, bursts of AK-47 gunfire crackled in the distance. These were fired by rebels celebrating their victory over Qaddafi, whose body lay some four hundred miles away in Misrata.

After a while, Malko went back into the house, then to his bedroom. When he lay down on the bed, Cynthia didn't even stir.

The convoy turned left and entered a walled compound.

General Younes could see parked vehicles and illuminated buildings: a militia base. His driver stopped, and the car was immediately surrounded by a dozen fierce-looking *thwars*. One opened the door on the general's side; two others opened the rear doors.

"Give me your weapons," snapped the first man.

A brief, tense silence followed. General Younes had his finger on his AK-47's trigger, but another AK was aimed at his belly. Controlling his fury, he gave the man his assault rifle.

The *thwar* pointed at Younes's belt.

"The pistol, too."

Younes took his 9 mm Makarov automatic from its holster and handed it over, holding it by the barrel. The two colonels in the back of the car also surrendered their weapons without resistance. The balance of power wasn't in their favor.

After disarming Younes's party, the bearded rebels stood around the car in complete silence.

Then a new man appeared, a *thwar* in a combat uniform with a pistol on his hip. To the driver he said:

"Get out. We don't need you anymore."

When the driver didn't react, the man grabbed his arm and

yanked him out of the car. A couple of *thwars* immediately surrounded him and dragged him off into the darkness.

A few seconds later, Younes was startled by the sound of three shots from the direction where his driver had been taken. A rebel was now sitting behind the wheel of the car.

"What's going on?" Younes asked him.

"I don't know," said the man, starting the engine.

Younes knew that something very serious was afoot. After all, he was the NTC chief of staff, and these militiamen should be obeying him.

They drove out of the camp and headed east on an empty road. The general's car was surrounded by a dozen armed pickups.

Trailing clouds of dust, they drove fast for about half an hour, then stopped in a stretch of empty, stony desert. The pickups pulled up in a semicircle around Younes's car. The rebel driver said:

"Get out, all of you."

The three officers obeyed. They were in the middle of nowhere, without a living soul in sight. Suddenly a Mercedes appeared, its doors adorned with the black, red, and green Libyan flag. It stopped, and a man got out. He was wearing a turban and a long white dishdasha, had a full black beard, and carried a folding AK-47. He walked up to the general and the two colonels.

Younes immediately recognized Abu Bukatalla. In a way, he was almost relieved. At last he was going to find out what was going on. Abu Bukatalla was the head of one of the NTC militias, so he was theoretically under Younes's command.

"Why was I brought here, and why was I disarmed?" Younes asked angrily. "Give me my pistol back. And where is my driver?"

The Islamist looked at him coldly.

"Your driver has been executed for the crimes he committed when he was interrogating our brothers in Abu Salim prison, on your orders." That was the biggest prison in Tripoli, which Qaddafi had filled with political prisoners.

Enraged, General Younes said:

"I've never been involved with the prison! I was the minister of defense!"

"Exactly. The prison was under you. You're the person who ordered twelve hundred prisoners executed, to please old 'Shafshufa.' Don't you remember?"

"I had nothing to do with that! I discussed it with NTC President Mustafa Abdel-Jalil before he gave me command of the liberation troops. I demand that you take me to him immediately."

Abu Bukatalla looked at Younes and said, "He's the person who told me to bring you here, judge you for your crimes, and execute you."

The general felt the blood draining from his face.

He understood.

"If you kill me, you'll pay for it in blood," he said. "My tribe is powerful and will avenge me."

Abu Bukatalla raised his right index finger to the sky.

"No one is more powerful than Allah the all-powerful and the all-merciful," he said sententiously. "You're nothing but a dog and a criminal. You killed your brothers, and you must die."

With that, he calmly raised his AK-47 and fired three-shot bursts, one at each prisoner.

General Younes and the two colonels crumpled in the dust. The militia leader turned to his men and said:

"Take their bodies to the ravine and burn them."

The *thwars* ran up and grabbed the corpses. But they were a little taken aback just the same. Under Islam, the dead are respected and bodies are never burned.

It is *haram*. A sin.

CHAPTER 17

Day was breaking.

The big farm northeast of Benghazi buzzed with feverish activity. The property, which belonged to a member of the Obeidi tribe, was the place where the group based its militia and stockpiled its weapons. Some fifteen armed pickup trucks were parked near the building that served as its headquarters.

Inside, the mood was unusually tense, as a half dozen men worked their phones trying to locate General Younes. An eminent member of the tribe, he'd been supposed to arrive the previous evening with a guest whose identity they didn't know, and spend the night at the base, protected by the tribe's fighters.

But they had waited all night, in vain. Younes had given no sign of life and wasn't answering his phone.

A tribesman hung up his cell phone and said:

"I just talked to Ra's Lanuf. The general left there yesterday around four in the afternoon with a small escort: a driver and two colonels from his general staff."

Another man spoke up:

"The NTC at Benghazi claims they're in the dark about this. President Abdel-Jalil is in Tripoli. It seems they got a phone call from the general last night saying he'd been intercepted by an armed group, but the man who took the call isn't there this morning."

The mood abruptly became more somber. Seated on a carpet on the ground, Fathi and Omar, two of Younes's nephews, felt a wave of anxiety.

"We have to investigate in town," said Fathi. "Somebody might have noticed something. Start with the Brega highway; he had to have driven that way. Question everybody, and especially at the checkpoints. Some of them are manned by people of the tribe."

That the general had probably been intercepted by armed men was a very bad sign. In an attempt to ward off fate, some of the tribesmen knelt and began to pray.

Ibrahim al-Senussi had fallen asleep very late, wracked with anxiety. The moment he woke up, he rushed to the terrace, pulled out his Thuraya, and dialed General Younes's number.

Without success.

He was feeling even more worried when he headed back downstairs and bumped into the young Islamist who brought him mint tea, water, and dates every morning. Though the young man's babyish face showed only the beginnings of a beard, he already had the fierce gaze of a God-crazed fanatic. Hand on his heart, he greeted al-Senussi politely:

"Salaam alaikum. I have a message for you."

"Alaikum salaam," said al-Senussi. "Is it from General Younes?"

"No, it's from Abu Bukatalla. He is coming to visit you soon. Inshallah, he will have important news for you."

Al-Senussi immediately relaxed. At last he would learn what had happened to General Younes. His tea and dates suddenly seemed to taste better.

Abd al-Raziq, Younes's favorite nephew, was tracking his uncle like a bloodhound. His investigation began at the Brega highway checkpoint south of Benghazi, the last one before reaching the city. It was manned by a member of the Watani tribe, and he gave al-Raziq his first lead. Yes, he said, a large convoy had passed the checkpoint: about twenty heavily armed pickups surrounding a Jeep Cherokee with the black, red, and green flag on its sides. The Watani man hadn't been able to see who was inside.

"Do you know who those people were?" asked al-Raziq.

"Yes. Emir Abu Bukatalla's brigade."

Al-Raziq's heart sank. They were his uncle's worst enemy.

"Where were they going?"

"Toward town."

Al-Raziq raced to Abu Bukatalla's old militia headquarters but found it deserted, its buildings ransacked and abandoned, and strewn with empty weapons crates.

On a hunch, he drove out on the Brega highway, stopping occasionally to ask questions at shops that were still open. From them, he learned that the convoy had gone around the city on one of the ring roads and then disappeared. No one had seen it travel beyond a certain intersection.

So they must have taken that fork, onto a dirt road leading east. There was no one left to question; they were now in open desert. Using his cell phone, al-Raziq roused a few loyalists, increasing his party's size to a dozen pickups and SUVs full of armed men.

The road wandered through the desert. Al-Raziq spotted a nomad camp and sent someone for information. The man came back a few moments later.

"They say they heard a convoy last night," he said, "but they don't know who it was."

There was nothing to do but follow the track as it snaked over the desert vastness. They were already about ten miles past Benghazi's Fifth Ring Road, and the track just went deeper into the desert without leading to a town or village.

Al-Raziq's group drove on until they came to a rise where the track petered out amid a jumble of sand dunes. On the ground, he could make out many tire tracks. A convoy had passed through here. What had they been doing in this desert dead end?

A fighter perched on top of one of the pickups said he could see something, a dark mound in a ravine.

Al-Raziq got out, his throat tight. He already knew what he was going to find.

The three bodies were unrecognizable, reduced to a charred black mass. Someone must have poured at least a jerry can of gasoline over them. It was impossible to tell how they died.

His heart as hard as flint, al-Raziq ordered a tarp brought and the remains of the three respectfully wrapped in it.

Given the state of the bodies, there was no way to positively identify them, but al-Raziq was sure they were his uncle and the two colonels. If he hadn't been so relentless in his search, they might have lain out here for weeks, and General Younes's fate would have remained a mystery. One often came across bodies of men executed in out-of-the-way places, without ever knowing what had happened. In these troubled times, there was no investigation. The corpses were simply buried.

Their grieving hearts full of hate, the men knelt on the stony ground, faced Mecca, and implored God Almighty to care for his dead servants.

There were now two things to be done: give these martyrs a decent burial, and avenge them.

Bursts of AK fire rang out, as his tribesmen gave General Younes a final salute.

By common accord, the convoy roared back toward town in a cloud of dust. Nobody said a word. The powerful Obeidi tribe had never been so humiliated.

This would be paid for in blood.

James Tuk, the State Department's representative in Benghazi, was in an office at NTC headquarters, a white, one-story building topped by the flag of the new Libya. He was discussing the possibility of releasing Libyan funds frozen in the United States.

Just then, several long bursts of AK-47 fire rattled outside and shattered several windows, including the one in the office where Tuk was speaking. He bravely ran to the window, to see that some twenty armed men had gotten out of their vehicles and were surrounding the building.

One of the men stepped forward and shouted something.

"He wants to talk to someone in charge," said Tuk, who understood Arabic.

They waited. A few more AK bursts rang out, chipping the stone facade. Quaking with fear, the council's general secretary went out to talk with the assailants. Their conversation was brief, and when the official was back inside, his colleagues immediately gathered around.

"They say that General Younes has been assassinated with the council's connivance," he managed to say. "I told them we didn't know anything about it, but they don't believe me."

"Do you think it's true?" asked the American dubiously.

Rumors travel fast in Libya.

"They offered to show me his body," said the official. "It's in one of the cars, along with two other men they found at the same time."

Tuk could hardly contain himself.

"I don't think this is a time to be talking finances," he said, apologizing to his interlocutor. "I have to report to my department."

The main supporter of American policy in Libya had just died.

That was very bad news.

From the window of his room overlooking al-Sharif, Ibrahim al-Senussi could see a dozen pickups blocking the narrow street. Armed with 23 mm cannons and full of men in a variety of outfits, they were parked right across from his house.

When he went downstairs, al-Senussi found the young Islamist coming to fetch him.

"The emir has arrived," he announced.

Abu Bukatalla was sitting down, leaning against some cushions. He had a folding AK-47 next to him and was drinking a glass of tea. He stood up to embrace al-Senussi, and the two men sat.

Al-Senussi immediately asked:

"Do you know where General Younes is?"

"I have bad news, brother," said the *takfiri* somberly.

"Has something happened to him?"

"No. When he learned that Qaddafi was dead, he left Ra's Lanuf and fled to the southwest, to Tuareg country."

Al-Senussi felt as if the sky had fallen on his head.

"Why would he do that?" he asked, his voice shaky.

"The NTC was secretly investigating him because he was suspected of maintaining relations with the other side. Younes had refused to launch certain offensives. He'd been summoned to Benghazi to explain himself, and he got frightened. I'm afraid we will never see him again. He is a traitor who hoped the situation would turn around. With Qaddafi dead, that's impossible."

Al-Senussi was crushed. General Younes was to be his major ally. He didn't know what to say.

"You should continue your consultations," said Abu Bukatalla, breaking the silence. "I'm sure there are other people you can talk to, likely supporters."

"Er, yes, of course," al-Senussi stammered, his mind in a whirl.

"You just need to adjust your plans," said the *takfiri* smoothly. "I have a few things to take care of, and I will be away for a day or two. When I get back, we'll see where we stand. I'm sure you'll find other allies to connect with."

Abu Bukatalla finished his tea and chewed a date, spitting out its pit. He stood, al-Senussi followed suit, and the two men embraced.

The Islamist chief left, escorted by four heavily armed militiamen. Moments later, the rumble of pickup truck engines broke the silence in the street, whose shops were still closed.

Feeling devastated, al-Senussi went back to his room. He didn't know what course to take.

General Younes was missing, but his Obeidi tribe was still one of the most powerful in eastern Libya. Its support would carry considerable political weight. Al-Senussi was also due to meet with members of the National Transitional Council. They didn't directly control any militias but were influential because of their political contacts abroad. The Western world had anointed the NTC as the leader of the new Libya, while realizing it was only a paper tiger.

The problem was, they didn't know about al-Senussi's presence in Benghazi. How would they view a secret trip organized under the auspices of a *takfiri* and British intelligence?

Al-Senussi was dying to call Cynthia to share his thinking, but he didn't know where she was.

Ted knocked at Malko's bedroom door. Cynthia was still asleep.

"I have a message for you," shouted the American. "You're to call Cairo."

Malko, who had just finished showering, took his satellite phone and went out on the lawn. The sky was still bright. Jerry Tombstone picked up on the first ring.

"I have some bad news," he drawled. "General Younes has been killed. The State Department just told me."

"Who did it?"

"We don't know yet, but probably the Islamists. I also spoke with the NTC president, who is in Tripoli. He hadn't even heard the news."

"So what does this mean?" asked Malko.

"That the next person on the list is our friend Ibrahim. Abu

Bukatalla had him come to Benghazi as a way of luring Younes out into the open. Now that al-Senussi's of no further use, he'll be the next to go."

"You think so?"

"If he isn't dead already," said Tombstone. "So we have two options: exfiltrate al-Senussi ASAP, or liquidate Abu Bukatalla. It would bother me to bring Ibrahim in from the cold. He might still be able to persuade other people to support him. Younes wasn't the only one. Besides, it's a long drive to the Egyptian border. It's more than four hundred miles, and you have to go through Derna, Abu Bukatalla's home turf."

"Can't we fly him out?"

"There aren't any flights before the weekend. The Agency could charter a plane, of course, but that would compromise him. So we're in deep shit. The best solution is to snatch him. We'll do what we discussed: throw Cynthia into the breach so we can contact Ibrahim and exfil him."

"And bring him here to the base?"

"I'll see what Langley says. We have to be careful not to compromise him too much. Go ahead with the plan."

Malko went back into the house. In the bedroom he found Cynthia awake but still in a fog.

"That was horrible, yesterday," she mumbled. "I've never been so scared in my life."

"You did great!" said Malko approvingly.

"I want to go back to Egypt," the young woman said, shaking her head. "This country's too dangerous."

"I understand your feelings. But first you have to do me a favor."

"What's that?"

"You're going to use my satellite phone and call Ibrahim. If his Thuraya isn't switched on, you'll leave a message asking him to call you back."

Cynthia stared at Malko in horror.

"You mean tell him I'm here?"

"I'm afraid so."

She shook her head again.

"He's going to kill me!"

"We'll keep him from doing that," said Malko. "But this is vital."

He handed her the Thuraya.

"Get up and come outside."

CHAPTER 18

Standing next to Cynthia out on the lawn, Malko listened as the Thuraya searched for a connection. When it succeeded, a recorded voice announced that the device they were calling was not in service. Malko took the sat phone, switched on the other Thuraya's voice mail, and gave it back to her.

"It's me," said Cynthia. "Ring me back on this number. It's extremely important. Love you."

She hung up and gave Malko the Thuraya.

"What do we do now?"

"We wait. Sit here on the steps so you can get a signal, and leave the phone switched on. I'll call Cairo to find out the next part of the operation."

"Do you think he'll call back?" she asked anxiously.

"I'm sure of it, but I don't know when."

"What shall I tell him?"

"That we have to get him out of where he is because his life is in danger. Don't go into detail. All he has to do is set a time when we can pick him up. Be convincing."

Malko went inside to the office where Ted had installed the communications links. The young American operative was working with one of the Marines.

"Send a man out to Cynthia," said Malko, "and have him tell me the moment the Thuraya rings. Meanwhile, I need to reach Cairo."

"This is a secure line," said Ted, handing him a satellite phone. "Go ahead."

Malko went back out to the lawn, which made the presence of the Marine unnecessary, since Cynthia was just a few feet away.

Jerry Tombstone must've been waiting for his call, because he picked up his direct line immediately.

"We phoned Ibrahim," Malko announced, "and we're waiting for him to call back. If he does, what do we do? Bring him here?"

"No," said the CIA station chief. "I discussed it with Langley and it's too risky politically. He would be connected to us. We'll put him somewhere else."

"Where?"

"In a hotel. Ted told me that there are lots of foreigners at the Ouzou and that the hotel is guarded by NTC *thwars*. That seems like a safe place. Abu Bukatalla can't very well go there to kill him. And once Ibrahim's safe, we'll have time to flush out the son of a bitch and get rid of him. If need be, you can do it with men of the Obeidi tribe. They'll kiss your hands."

The communication ended, Malko went over to sit by Cynthia on the steps in the sunshine.

"I've spoken to Cairo," he said, "and they don't want Ibrahim to come here. Too dangerous politically. So we'll set him up at the Ouzou Hotel, guarded by CIA men. The hotel is controlled by the National Transitional Council."

"But he still hasn't called," she objected.

"Let's hope he does," said Malko with a sigh.

She turned to him.

"If he agrees, what do I do? Do I go with him?"

"I'm afraid that's going to be necessary," he said diplomatically. "You'll be the carrot."

The young woman glared at him.

"Bastard! You don't care about me."

"That's not true," Malko assured her. "But my overriding goal is to keep Ibrahim alive, regardless of my personal feelings."

She was furious, but she dropped the subject.

"Anyway, he hasn't called."

Ibrahim al-Senussi was listening to Cynthia Mulligan's message for the third time, torn between the joy of hearing her voice and anxiety. What did this call mean? He'd been shattered by what Abu Bukatalla told him about General Younes, and now he was paralyzed with indecision. After hesitating a long time, he dialed the unknown satellite phone, his throat tight.

He was standing on the little terrace, his pulse racing as he waited.

The seconds slowly ticked by until his phone finally connected to the satellite and dialed the number.

When al-Senussi heard a female voice say "Hello?" he thought his heart would stop.

"Cynthia?"

"Yes, it's me," said the young woman. "I'm so glad you called me back!"

"Where are you?"

"In Benghazi."

"In Benghazi?" Al-Senussi couldn't believe his ears. "What are you doing in Benghazi?"

"I can explain everything," she said. "But you have to listen to me. You're in mortal danger. I'm calling you to save your life."

Completely at a loss, al-Senussi protested, "I'm not in any danger! Where did you get that satellite phone? Why did you leave Cairo?"

"I'll explain everything," Cynthia repeated, "but you have to believe me. General Younes, the man you were planning to meet, has been killed. And he was killed by Abu Bukatalla, the man who's supposed to be protecting you."

Al-Senussi couldn't believe what he was hearing. How did Cynthia know all those names? He had never told her anything.

"That's not true! General Younes wasn't killed. He ran away. He's a traitor."

"Call Herbert Mallows in Cairo. He'll confirm it."

Al-Senussi had never told Cynthia the name of the MI6 agent in Cairo, either.

Interrupting his train of thought, she said:

"Listen, we'll talk about all this later. Are you free to move around al-Sharif Street?"

Al-Senussi was speechless. How in the world did she know where he was? Cynthia's voice reached him as if in a dream.

"Can you go out or not?" she asked.

"Of course I can. Why?"

"In an hour, a white SUV will stop across from where you

are. I'll be inside, with some people who will be protecting you. As soon as I see you on the sidewalk, I'll come meet you."

"Are you mad? To go where?"

"To a safe place. I'm counting on you. Otherwise. I'm afraid we'll never see each other again."

There was a click, and the line went dead.

Al-Senussi glared at his Thuraya reproachfully, as if it were responsible for the break in communication. Then he folded its antenna and went downstairs, his mind in a whirl. He didn't know what was going on.

Sitting on his bed, he put his head in his hands. How could Cynthia know all those things? Then a terrible thought occurred to him. What if British intelligence had put her on his path, as a way to control him? But his questions were swept away by jealousy. Whom had she come to Benghazi with?

He looked at his watch: it was 10:55. If Cynthia was telling the truth, she would be there in less than an hour. He didn't believe this business about his life being in danger, but he felt overwhelmed by the desire to see the young Englishwoman again.

After all, he could go to the meeting, get her, and see what developed.

He had fifty-five minutes to make up his mind.

Cynthia shot Malko a dark look.

"Happy now?" she demanded.

"You were perfect!" he assured her. "And you're going to help us save Ibrahim's life."

"I don't give a damn about Ibrahim."

She felt guilty about going along with this plan just to please the man she'd fallen in love with. And now that man, for some inexplicable reason, was coldly sending her back to her old lover's arms.

"We'll be going soon," said Malko.

His eye caught Cynthia's, and the young woman thought she'd felt an electric shock in her groin. She realized that she was completely aroused and that her thighs were parting of their own accord. If Malko had taken her right there on the steps in front of everybody, she wouldn't have resisted.

But Cynthia's pride was stronger.

"Very well," she said coldly. "I'll get my things together. I don't suppose I'll be coming back here afterward, will I?"

"That's right."

She walked into the villa without turning around, and Malko followed her with his eyes. He would happily have made love to her, but just then he had other fish to fry, alas. He stepped into the office where Ted was waiting.

"We'll go in ten minutes," he announced.

The two Cherokees drove out the gate and turned right. Ted was driving the lead car, with Malko sitting next to him. Cynthia, looking attractive in fresh makeup and jeans, was in the back, seated next to a Marine with a shaved head.

The second, protection, car carried four heavily armed special-ops men.

Cynthia leaned forward to speak to Malko.

"If Ibrahim comes out, what do I do next?"

"We'll go to the Ouzou Hotel, where we'll check you in. Two of our men will stay with you."

"And after that?"

"After that, we'll see. One bridge at a time."

The two SUVs stopped before reaching the 23rd July Lake Bridge. Malko got out and moved to the second car, trading places with a gum-chewing, square-jawed Marine who wasn't likely to spark al-Senussi's jealousy.

Ten minutes later, they turned into al-Sharif Street. The lead Cherokee, with Cynthia, passed Masawi Street and stopped twenty yards beyond it. Malko's car stopped short of the intersection, in front of a shoe store that was opening for business.

It was 11:55.

Traffic in the street was fairly heavy, but nobody seemed to pay any attention to their two cars.

They had five minutes to go.

Malko was as taut as a violin string. If al-Senussi didn't come out, it would be difficult to go inside to get him. He might be held against his will or, on the contrary, not willing to leave his hiding place. In that case, the plan would fail.

He stiffened: someone had just emerged from the house with the armed pickup truck parked in front. Malko could see him only from behind, but the man was wearing a Western suit and heading for the end of al-Sharif Street, where it met the corniche.

Just then, a door of the lead Cherokee opened and Cynthia stepped out onto the sidewalk. She stood motionless for a moment, then walked toward the man who had come out of the house.

Malko held his breath as the two people got closer. The man threw himself into Cynthia's arms.

Just at that moment, two militiamen with AK-47s burst out of the house and ran screaming toward the couple embracing on the sidewalk.

CHAPTER 19

Malko cursed: everything was falling apart. But just then, one of the Marines in the lead car with Cynthia jumped out and fired a warning burst from his M16. The two militiamen with Kalashnikovs froze. Malko watched as al-Senussi shoved Cynthia into the Cherokee, climbed in, and slammed the door behind them. Keeping his eye on the two men, the Marine fired another burst in the air and got back into the car.

The militiamen could have shot at the Cherokee, but they didn't. Instead, they ran back into the house.

Malko's car started up, and by the time it passed the building where al-Senussi had been housed, the Cherokee ahead of them had reached the end of al-Sharif Street. None of the passersby had paid much attention to the gunfire. In Benghazi, you heard it all the time.

The lead Cherokee turned right, heading around the Old City toward the Ouzou Hotel on the other side of 23rd July Lake. Malko's SUV followed as far as the turnoff to the hotel, whose entrance was still guarded by *thwars* under the big umbrella with the new Libya colors.

"We're going home," he told his driver, feeling reassured.

For the time being, Ibrahim al-Senussi was safe.

Without really thinking, al-Senussi took Cynthia's hand.

"Where are we going?" he asked vacantly.

"To the Ouzou Hotel," answered Ted, who was driving.

The Libyan was puzzled. Why a hotel? All he could think of was being alone with Cynthia to straighten out what was happening.

They passed through the *thwar* checkpoint without any trouble, and a Marine took Cynthia's suitcase and they entered the hotel.

Ted turned to al-Senussi and said, "Give me your passport, sir. I'll check you in with us. We'll be in the rooms on either side of yours."

Journalists of every nationality sat sprawled around the Ouzou's various public rooms, reading or typing on laptops. The hotel was clean, modern, and soulless.

The Ouzou's foreign employees had fled during the revolution, and the hotel was doing the best it could with local staff, who spoke only Arabic and weren't very professional. The desk clerk carefully kept the guests' passports to prevent people from skipping out on their bills.

Using all his Arabic, Ted negotiated a deposit of five hundred dinars in exchange for being able to keep Ibrahim's passport. The clerk registered the Libyan without comment. The name al-Senussi was a common one, and in his eyes, Ibrahim was a guest like any other.

The formalities completed, Ted handed al-Senussi his magnetic room key.

"You're in Room 407, sir. We're in 406 and 408. We'll go upstairs with you."

Still under the shock of his "kidnapping," al-Senussi didn't protest.

The four of them crammed into one of the elevators. Upstairs, the once-pink hall carpet now showed nothing but stains.

Al-Senussi's room was small and Spartan, with a big air conditioner and a tiny bathroom.

He collapsed on the bed, suddenly exhausted.

"I don't have a change of clothes!" he moaned. "I left everything back there."

"We'll buy you whatever you need," promised Cynthia. "Do you want to take a nap?"

"A nap? I want to find out what's going on, and especially what you're doing in Benghazi. Why did you lie to me?"

They hadn't said a word to each other in the car. Cynthia, who had been carefully briefed by Malko, sat down on the bed beside her lover.

"It's a little complicated," she admitted. "After you left Cairo, I was approached by a man who said he was a CIA agent. He took me to the American embassy, where I met his boss, a bloke named Gerald Tombstone. He explained that the CIA was working with MI6 on a political operation designed to give you an important position in the new Libya."

Al-Senussi listened in astonishment. Everything Cynthia was saying was true.

The young woman continued:

"They also told me that the plane we took to Cairo was nearly shot down by a surface-to-air missile. Luckily, it didn't go off."

"What?" The Libyan was startled. "I didn't see a thing."

"Yes, but it was true. The Egyptians found the unexploded missile. This proved to the English and the Americans that there were people in Libya who wanted to get rid of you, because you were an obstacle to their plans."

"What plans?"

"Qatar's plans," she continued. "The emir of Qatar wants to set up a strict Islamist regime in Libya, relying on the various Islamist groups that are active here. One of them is led by Abu Bukatalla. Apparently he's a *takfiri*, the most radical kind of Islamist."

"Abu Bukatalla . . . ," murmured al-Senussi in a dull voice. "His representative in London swore that he was prepared to support me. He's the one who asked me to come to Cairo. But if what you're saying is true, why not kill me right away after the first attempt?"

"Because he needed you to lure General Younes into a trap. Younes was the Islamists' mortal enemy."

"General Younes ran away with Qaddafists," al-Senussi snapped.

"That's not true," said Cynthia. "He was killed when he was on his way to meet you. You're the only person who doesn't know it. The NTC is investigating his death. If you want to check, you can call Herbert Mallows in Cairo."

"Did you meet him, too?" he asked, astonished.

"No, they just gave me his name. Abu Bukatalla is double-crossing you. And now that General Younes is dead, you're living on borrowed time. That's why the Americans picked you up."

"This is all crazy!" said the Libyan, shaking his head. "I have to talk to Abu Bukatalla. I'm sure he has an explanation."

Cynthia started.

"You know where he is?" she quickly asked.

"No, I don't," al-Senussi admitted. Then he caught himself and gave her a hard look. "This doesn't explain why you lied to me. Why did you come to Benghazi?"

"To save your life," said the young woman simply. "The Americans didn't know where you were, or if you would accept a phone call from someone you didn't know. But they knew you would answer me.

"They located you thanks to your satellite phone. They asked me to help them, and that's why I phoned. If you hadn't seen me on the street, I bet you wouldn't have come out."

Al-Senussi shook his head again. He was feeling overwhelmed.

"Are you staying at this hotel?" he asked.

"No. The Americans put me up at their base. But I'll stay here with you, if you like."

"If I like! I haven't seen you for days. I didn't know where you were. I thought you'd gone off with another man."

"Well, I didn't! In Cairo I went with the Americans from the CIA. Then I flew here on a U.N. plane and they put me up in a villa on their base. It's a beautiful place."

"Why didn't they bring me to where you're staying?" al-Senussi asked suspiciously.

Cynthia gave him a disarming smile.

"Because it's an official U.S. State Department residence. It would compromise you."

"What about the British?"

"We're working hand in glove with the Americans."

Al-Senussi was staring at Cynthia. His fear and surprise had almost disappeared, replaced by a renewed taste for life. Watching the young woman's breasts moving under her blouse, he felt his blood rising.

"You're as beautiful as ever," he said in a voice husky with desire.

His hand had already grabbed at Cynthia's pants, fondling her crotch through the fabric.

He couldn't help himself.

He didn't even bother kissing her. Clothes went flying in a confused melee. Cynthia had been expecting the outburst and didn't fight it. She just tried to replace the Libyan's image with that of the man she had fallen in love with.

Al-Senussi shoved her thighs apart with his knee and plunged into her, his cock ready to explode. Biting her lip, Cynthia closed her eyes.

Abu Bukatalla was having trouble mastering his rage. Stationed with some thirty of his men at the farm outside Benghazi, he had just learned of al-Senussi's flight—and couldn't understand it.

The pretender to the Libyan throne had always listened to him and seemed to trust him.

To complete the task assigned by his sponsors in Cairo, Abu Bukatalla just had two more things to do: eliminate the leader of the Obeidi tribe and kill Ibrahim al-Senussi. He'd done the first, and getting rid of al-Senussi should be easy. Since there weren't any flights to Cairo, he would have to be driven there. All Abu Bukatalla had to do was to set up an ambush.

The way would then be clear for whomever the various Libyan Islamist leaders and the emir of Qatar selected. Abu

Bukatalla was counting on playing a major role in the new government, which would receive billions of dollars in Libyan assets frozen by the United States. The Americans were reluctant to turn them over to the NTC, whose weakness was obvious.

The *takfiri* leader had promised himself that he would use some of those funds to support jihad in Africa through al-Qaeda in the Islamic Maghreb, which lacked weapons and money. His goal was clear: establishing an Islamic caliphate in Libya that would apply sharia law with absolute strictness. Once that foundation was established, Abu Bukatalla would be able to help his brothers in jihad in their struggle against the hated infidels.

And now that beautiful plan was in danger of falling apart. To get al-Senussi back, Abu Bukatalla would have to trick him. But first he had to find out where he was.

It was fortunate that there weren't any planes available, though the Americans could still get him out by road, with an armed escort and NATO support.

Abu Bukatalla ate a few dates, then called one of his men.

"Go out to the American base and keep an eye on it," he said. "If al-Senussi's still in Benghazi, that's where he'll be."

Attacking the base would be very risky, except maybe at night. The CIA men were armed and trained, and they would know how to defend themselves.

The *takfiri* leader had just finished his tea when his cell phone rang. It was one of his contacts at the Ouzou Hotel, who told him that a Libyan man and a foreign woman had just checked in, protected by two Americans.

Abu Bukatalla blessed the name of Allah: he had located

al-Senussi! The two militiamen guarding the Libyan at the safe house said he'd met a woman and run off with her. It was now up to Abu Bukatalla to make his move. A direct assault on the hotel was out of the question, so he had to devise a ruse to draw al-Senussi out of hiding—and kill him.

CHAPTER 20

"The NTC just announced that it had nothing to do with General Younes's death," said Ted, holding a press release that had just gone out on the Net.

"I'm going to contact Cairo," said Malko. "Is Ibrahim settled at the Ouzou?"

"Looks that way," said the American. "Our two guys are with him."

"Great. I'll talk to Cairo and see where we stand."

Al-Senussi's stay at the Ouzou was only temporary, and they had to decide what to do next. Malko felt a twinge, thinking about Cynthia. He went back out onto the sun-splashed lawn, the only place where his Thuraya worked.

"The situation's under control," he told Tombstone. "Ibrahim is safe at the Ouzou. We just have to exfiltrate him from Benghazi."

"Not yet," the American objected. "We're going to try to capitalize on General Younes's murder. The Obeidi tribe has sided with us from the very beginning, and now they're furious at the Islamists. Ted's been in touch with them. I'll ask him to set up a meeting with the head of the tribe, through the general's nephew, Abd al-Raziq. If they decide to support Ibrahim, we'll be able to exfil him."

"You think that'll be enough?"

"Frankly, no," Tombstone admitted, "but at least we'll have that much. And there's another matter to settle: Abu Bukatalla. Qatar wants a puppet Islamist state, and as Qatar's muscle, he could be a major nuisance.

"The NTC is too weak to do anything against him, so I'm putting you in charge of the problem. You'll earn yourself some friends among the Cousins. They haven't gotten over Peter Farnborough's killing."

"But I don't know where Abu Bukatalla is," objected Malko.

"You said that NGO staffer Manuela Esteban is coming back to Benghazi today, right? Maybe she can help you pick up his trail."

"I'll try," promised Malko, "but the special-ops men aren't eager to mount an operation against him."

"They'll follow orders," said the station chief sharply. "Anyway, if you find Abu Bukatalla, you can count on the Obeidi. They have a debt of honor to settle with him, and people here don't kid around with that sort of thing. I'm relying on you."

As he went back to the lounge, Malko understood two things. First, the Ibrahim al-Senussi project was in trouble. Second, Abu Bukatalla had become a personal matter for the Agency and the Cousins. The Anglo-Saxons didn't just honor their dead; they avenged them.

To find Manuela Esteban, Malko had to go to the Ouzou, where he might bump into al-Senussi and Cynthia—and that could be a big problem. The Libyan had seen him in Cairo. If he saw him again in Benghazi, he might start to ask himself questions and figure out that Malko was the person who had brought Cynthia to Libya.

If Ibrahim tumbled to that, it could seriously screw up the CIA operation.

Luckily, a solution occurred to him. Ted could take al-Senussi out to a meeting with General Younes's nephew al-Raziq. Malko could then go to the Ouzou, sure that he wouldn't run into him.

He just had to get the timing right.

Al-Senussi was sitting in one of the deep leather armchairs in a study off the Ouzou lobby. He couldn't take his hand off Cynthia's thigh as she chastely perched in the chair next to his.

Ted was trying not to look at them.

A conservative Christian, he considered these public displays of intimacy very distasteful. So did the Libyans nearby, who felt that in a properly run country the sinner's hand would be chopped off. It was hard to believe that the young woman didn't have a brother, father, or cousin to exterminate this sex-crazed scum.

"We have an appointment with Abd al-Raziq, General Younes's nephew," said Ted, who had just arrived at the Ouzou. "He'll be accompanied by representatives of the Obeidi tribe. It'll be up to you to convince them to support you."

Bounced back and forth between people who all seemed to be playing a double game, the Libyan no longer knew which way to turn. He would have preferred to spend the afternoon with Cynthia, but he understood that the American planned to stick with him.

"Can I bring my girlfriend?" he asked.

"No, sir," said Ted, managing to keep his composure. "It wouldn't be appropriate."

That was a major understatement. In Libya, nobody would dream of bringing a woman to an important meeting.

Al-Senussi was mulling over Ted's answer when his cell phone rang. An unknown number.

"Whatever happened to you, brother?" asked Abu Bukatalla in honeyed tones. "I was told you were kidnapped by foreigners. Where are you? And why didn't you let me know?"

Fortunately, al-Senussi now knew whom he was dealing with. Ted had just shown him the NTC communiqué about General Younes's death. So instead of confronting the Islamist, he pretended to be apologetic.

"I wasn't kidnapped," he said. "I wanted to see my girlfriend, who just arrived from Cairo. I'm at the Ouzou Hotel."

"I need to see you. I'll send a car for you."

"I can't right now," said al-Senussi. "I have an important meeting."

Ted scrawled on a newspaper: *Tell him who it's with.*

"Who are you seeing?" asked Abu Bukatalla.

"Representatives of the Obeidi tribe, at the house of Abd al-Raziq, General Younes's nephew. They asked to meet with me."

A brief silence followed. Then Abu Bukatalla spoke:

"Good, good," he said smoothly. "That's encouraging."

"Why don't you come have tea with me at the hotel later today?" suggested al-Senussi.

"That's an excellent idea. I'll come one hour before evening prayers, and we can go together."

"Inshallah, until this evening," said Ibrahim before hanging up.

Ted gave him a wicked grin.

"Well done!" he said approvingly. "We're gonna rock 'n' roll today."

"What do you mean?" asked al-Senussi, looking at him quizzically.

"I'll bet a pizza against a pound of caviar that the son of a bitch will try to kill two birds with one stone—terminating you while taking out some of his worst enemies."

"I better not go to that meeting," the Libyan concluded.

"Oh no, just the opposite! We're going to spring a little surprise on them. C'mon upstairs, and we'll outfit you."

Cynthia watched anxiously as al-Senussi was fitted with a Kevlar GK bulletproof vest that Ted had taken from a sport bag.

Al-Senussi was looking a little green around the gills. When the British originally suggested that he could be the next king of Libya, he'd found the idea very attractive. He'd imagined leisurely chats, with lots of tea and cakes, with friendly, civilized people.

Not ferocious killers bent on assassinating him.

Ted, who under his photographer's vest carried a .357 Magnum automatic that could kill an elephant, hustled him out of the room.

"Let's roll!" he said, flashing a smile at Cynthia. "We'll bring him back in one piece, miss."

The Englishwoman, who was learning about the new world she'd been thrown into, wasn't so sure. She merely smiled tightly and planted a kiss on her lover's dry lips.

Downstairs, al-Senussi found four more Americans in the

lobby. Two unmarked Cherokees were parked in front of the hotel, with yet more Marines aboard.

Everybody piled into the cars, and the convoy took off down Algeria Street. Each Cherokee was as heavily armed as a small aircraft carrier, with RPGs stowed on the floor for safety.

Ted dialed a number on his cell.

"We're leaving the hotel," he said briefly. "ETA in thirty."

Al-Senussi couldn't hear the answer, which was just as well. Ted was talking to General Younes's nephew Fathi, who had assembled twenty heavily armed pickups near the villa where al-Senussi was heading.

The trucks had 23 mm cannons and Dushka machine guns manned by Obeidi tribesmen all bent on avenging the murdered general. They were prepared to risk their lives if it meant wiping out their enemies. This mattered a lot more than tracking down former Qaddafists. In Libya, debts of blood were paid in full, and with interest.

Squeezed between two husky Marines, al-Senussi watched the flat landscape with its walled estates roll by. To avoid imagining what might happen in the coming hours, he tried to think about Cynthia. His convoy's show of strength didn't fully reassure him. He knew the *takfiri* Islamists' ferocity and their willingness to sacrifice their lives to attain their goal.

Even if the Americans killed them all, it wouldn't do al-Senussi much good if he wound up with a bullet in his head.

The convoy slowed. They were now in an upscale neighborhood, with beautiful houses protected by high walls, and no pedestrians. Only rich people lived here.

As they waited for the gate to open, al-Senussi saw a little red Hyundai come out of a neighboring property. It was driven by a very pretty brunette with full lips, her head barely covered by a purple scarf.

Heavenly.

The Cherokee entered the property. A young man waiting on the front steps hugged al-Senussi, kissing him twice on the shoulder as a sign of respect.

Inside, the residence was luxurious, with new furniture and hangings everywhere. The place was so neat, you'd almost think it was a model apartment. A dozen men were sitting on the floor along the walls, leaning on embroidered cushions: the representatives of the Obeidi tribe. The nephew handled the introductions, and Ted discreetly slipped out.

He had to be ready for a possible attack by Abu Bukatalla.

Malko passed through the Ouzou's metal detector and headed for the front desk. There was no one there, so he took the elevator and knocked on the door of Room 315, the room of Manuela Esteban, Peter Farnborough's friend.

No answer.

The door of the room across the way was open, and Malko could see a couple of people working, NGO staffers or journalists. One of them called out to him:

"You looking for Manuela?"

"Yes."

"She went to the front, to teach mine clearing. She'll be back later."

Malko thanked him and went back to the elevator. But when the doors opened, he got a shock: there stood Cynthia, looking demure in a heavy blouse and jeans.

The surprise was mutual.

"Were you looking for me?" she immediately asked as he stepped in.

"No," said Malko. "I don't want to play with fire."

"Ibrahim isn't here. He went to a meeting with your friends. And in that case, what are you doing here?"

"I'm trying to find whoever killed an MI6 agent. But the person I wanted to see wasn't there."

The elevator jerked to a stop at the ground floor, and Malko stepped aside to let the young woman pass.

"We have to talk," she said, planting herself in front of him.

"It's too risky here."

Cynthia paid no heed.

"Look," she said in a contained voice that shook with anger. "If you don't listen to me, I swear I'm taking a taxi back to Egypt. I can't stand this anymore."

Malko weighed the young woman's expression. There was no doubt that she was talking seriously, and if she carried out her threat, al-Senussi would be impossible to control.

"Okay, let's go to the restaurant. If Ibrahim comes in, just say I'm part of the CIA team here."

Cynthia gave him an ironic look as she led him into the empty dining room.

"You're forgetting that he saw you at the Four Seasons. You'll have to come up with a different story."

Choosing a table off to the side, Malko kept his eyes on the entrance. If al-Senussi found him in Cynthia's company, he might guess the truth, and it would be all over.

The CIA's plans were already limping. Malko didn't have much time to convince the young woman not to scuttle them.

CHAPTER 21

The croissants could have been baked with rock flour, the coffee was swill, and there was nothing to eat but hard-boiled eggs and jam made from some extraterrestrial fruit.

Cynthia took a tiny sip of her coffee and looked straight at Malko.

"I can't stand Ibrahim anymore," she said. "I want to go back with you."

That was unexpected and flattering.

"Later," said Malko diplomatically. "You have to stay with him for the time being. Just hang on for a couple of days. Ibrahim is trying to convince some important tribal chiefs to support him. And Abu Bukatalla is on the prowl. I'm sure he'll try to kill him."

"Why doesn't Ibrahim just go back to Egypt?"

"There aren't any flights, and traveling by road is too dangerous. Abu Bukatalla has to be eliminated before he can attack Ibrahim. That's what I'm here for."

"When will that happen?"

"If I only knew!" said Malko with a smile. "First I have to find where he's hiding."

Cynthia was silent for a few moments; then she said:

"Well, I'll stay, but not for long. And you have to do something."

"What?"

"Come up to my room with me. Ibrahim won't be coming back right away."

Malko could feel goose bumps on the backs of his hands.

"No," he said firmly. "I can't do that."

The British woman didn't give up.

"In that case, take me to your friends' villa for a while. You have a car, don't you?"

Cynthia put her hand on his and dug her nails into his skin. With a sly smile, she said:

"I want you to eat me."

Driven only by female instinct, she wasn't about to let him off the hook, Malko realized. She didn't give a damn about al-Senussi's royal projects. Malko had apparently opened a Pandora's box.

"All right, but we can't stay long," he said. "Ibrahim will be looking for you everywhere."

"I'll say I went shopping," she said, standing up.

Malko shook his head, feeling discouraged.

"There isn't any shopping here! Tell him you went to change some money in the Old City."

He prayed that al-Senussi's meeting would last a little longer.

A dozen pickup trucks crammed with men and outfitted with automatic weapons that could shatter walls, including a 23 mm cannon, were parked at an abandoned farm on the Third Ring Road. Abu Bukatalla was in the rear compartment of the first vehicle, which was equipped with a quad-barrel antiaircraft gun.

With this much firepower at his disposal, Abu Bukatalla could easily blow away the Americans protecting al-Senussi. The field would then be open for the Islamist camp. Qatar would gladly support the first candidate he named, and the man would be elected easily. Alternately, when the next government was formed, the Islamists could arrange to control all the key positions.

Thanks to Qatar, which supplied all the gasoline consumed in Libya, Abu Bukatalla was in a strong bargaining position.

His cell rang.

"They've arrived," said the lookout whom he had stationed near Abd-al-Raziq's villa. "The infidels have two vehicles positioned at the ends of the street. Others are inside, with him."

"*Shukran*," said Abu Bukatalla, thanking him. "We'll be there soon. When you see us coming, attack one of the infidels' vehicles."

"*Allahu akbar!*" said the *takfiri* in a throbbing voice.

The column of pickups pulled out of the farm and took the Third Ring Road, heading west.

In Benghazi, nobody was surprised to encounter such a convoy. You saw them all the time, heading for the front or returning from it. Nobody controlled the movements of the various militias, which were fiercely jealous of their independence; there was no central command or military police since General Younes's death, and anyone flying the flag of the revolution could display weapons. So Abu Bukatalla didn't risk running into any problems.

They ran three red lights in a row—no one would dispute the right of way with such a powerful armada—and reached the al-Mhayshi suburb. This was a neighborhood of luxurious properties belonging to Qaddafi supporters who had quietly amassed large fortunes during the forty-two years of his rule.

Abu Bukatalla saw his lookout leaning against a wall, just before the corner of the next street. When the man saw the militia pickups, he shouldered an RPG-7, kneeled, and took aim at the Cherokee blocking the road to the villa.

Cynthia and Malko had reached the Ouzou's metal detector and were passing the "guards" sprawled on old leather sofas when a group of a half dozen men and women came into the hotel. One of them was an unusually small, energetic-looking woman wearing boots and a field jacket and holding an antitank mine—almost certainly a dummy—in her right hand.

Malko felt his pulse start to race.

"Are you Manuela Esteban?" he asked.

She looked up in surprise.

"Yes, I am. Do I know you?"

"No. I was a good friend of Peter Farnborough."

"But Peter—"

"—is dead, I know. That's why I'm here. Can we talk?"

"Sure. I'll just take this up to my room."

"May I come with you?" asked Malko.

Esteban quickly looked him over and decided there was nothing sexual in his request.

"*Bueno*," she said. "Follow me."

Malko took a moment to run over to Cynthia, who was standing uncertainly in the middle of the lobby.

"This is the person I wanted to see," he said. "Go back up to your room and I'll come for you."

He got into the elevator just in time. The tiny Spanish woman came up only to his shoulder, but she might be able to help him find Abu Bukatalla.

“They’re attacking!” said Ted into his cell.

He was answered with a roar of joy. The Obeidi tribesmen were gathered three streets away, in pickups like Abu Bukatalla’s, galvanized by the idea of avenging General Younes. As their first pickup started up, the 23 mm gunner fired a short burst in the air to make sure his twin guns were working properly. A few minutes later, it was facing a pickup truck flying the white flag of Abu Bukatalla’s militia. In front of them, the Cherokee hit by the RPG-7 grenade was burning.

The Americans had cautiously taken positions inside the villa.

The two pickup trucks reacted in exactly the same way, slewing broadside to the street so their automatic weapons could fire on their adversaries.

For a few moments, nothing could be heard over the deafening boom-boom-boom of the 23 mm cannons as their shells tore the two vehicles to pieces.

In any civilized city, neighbors would have rushed to the phone to call the police. But Benghazi had no police and many Qaddafists in hiding, so the fight might well be a legitimate one.

Abruptly, silence fell. The drawback of these automatic weapons was that their magazines emptied quickly when they were fired in long bursts. Another firefight broke out a little farther down the street as Obeidi pickups attacked the rear of Abu Bukatalla’s column.

The first two vehicles to face off were now ablaze, and their occupants all dead or wounded, including the gunners. The 23 mm barrels pointed uselessly at the sky.

Abu Bukatalla, who had been lying low from the start of the attack, jumped out into the street while it was still protected and climbed into another pickup. He was furious. How did the Americans know he was planning to attack? He gave some orders on his cell, and the armed pickups began to withdraw. Disengagement had always been one of the militias' strong points.

Greatly outnumbered by its adversaries, one pickup sacrificed itself to slow them down.

As he fled, Abu Bukatalla raged. He'd been unmasked in Ibrahim al-Senussi's eyes. King Idris's grandson now knew that the *takfiri* wanted to kill him. He would have to make a new attempt to get rid of this American pawn while he was still in Benghazi.

At whatever cost.

The detonations were becoming fewer, muffled by the house's thick walls.

Al-Senussi was lying behind a heavy sofa, screened by the body of a CIA operative. Other Americans and Obeidi tribesmen were positioned in the rooms and the garden, but the battle never got that far.

Finally, silence fell.

Ted had been communicating by radio with his men outside throughout the battle. He now turned to the Libyan and said, "They're running away! They lost three vehicles and quite a few men."

"And you're really sure it was Abu Bukatalla?" asked al-Senussi.

Ted was incredulous. They kept telling al-Senussi that the Islamists planned to kill him and had already tried when he was landing in Cairo, yet he still couldn't believe it.

"Yes, it was," he said. "Unfortunately, he got away. But the dead are there, and we can identify them."

Al-Senussi stood up, dazed. He was handed a glass of hot tea, which he took and gulped down.

"What am I supposed to do now?"

He was answered by an old man with a beard, the head of the Obeidi tribe.

"Take power and kill those bad Muslims," he said coldly. "Those God crazies think they know the Quran better than we do. Then bring peace to Libya, inshallah."

Al-Senussi didn't answer. At the moment, he mainly wanted to go back to the Ouzou and Cynthia. He didn't feel at all cut out to be a king.

Sitting on Manuela Esteban's bed, Malko listened as the young mine clearer told her story. She'd been reticent at first, until he convinced her that she could help him find Farnborough's killers.

"I know how Peter got the information he was looking for," she said. "It was through me."

"How so?"

"At the arms bazaar, I was buying beer from an old Chadian, a Toubou who also sells weapons. He'd told me he got the guns from Abu Bukatalla's militia. Peter asked to meet him, and I took him to his stand in the market. I didn't hear what they talked about, but when we left, Peter said he had a meeting the next day with someone who would lead him to Abu Bukatalla."

"And the next day we found Peter killed," continued Malko. "So this man betrayed him."

"Yes, probably."

"Would you recognize him?"

"Sure, but I don't know his name."

"But you know where he is in the market?

"Yes, he's always at the same place, not far from Syria Street."

"When could we see him?"

Esteban hesitated, then looked at her watch.

"The market should be open now, but it's dangerous. I don't know if—"

"Let's go there," said Malko. "You don't need to show yourself. All you have to do is point the man out to me. After that, you can leave."

After a short silence, she agreed.

"*Bueno*, I'll go with you. I was very fond of Peter."

CHAPTER 22

The market occupied a broad esplanade between Algeria and Syria Streets in the Assilmani neighborhood north of the city, not far from the sea. Hundreds of cars were scattered in a makeshift parking lot. The CIA agent driving Malko parked their blue Ford on Syria Street, ready to take off. Malko got out, with Manuela Esteban on his heels.

One thing struck him immediately: the silence, despite the hundreds of people on the square—merchants, buyers, and others strolling the improvised alleyways.

It was like a huge flea market.

At one stand, a trestle displayed handguns, empty magazines, a couple of AK-47s, even an ancient Schmeisser submachine gun from Afrika Korps days.

Along the alleys, people were talking quietly, and the merchants didn't appear to be hustling their customers. Everything took place in a kind of muffled silence. It was eerie.

Malko turned to the young Spanish woman and asked, "Which way is it?"

"That way, in the back. I hope he's there."

As they walked, they encountered looks of surprise but not hostility. Malko happened to notice a man take a six-pack of Heineken beer out of a crate. Meeting Malko's eye, he ran off in shame, as if he'd been caught with child pornography.

The prevailing mood was sober. It felt like people were on their guard.

"Do the police ever come here?" he asked.

"What police? There aren't any in Benghazi, and the traffic cops aren't armed."

They continued walking. There weren't any sophisticated weapons to be seen, not even RPGs, but maybe you had to ask for them. There was a lot of ammunition, quite a few handguns, some of them unusual, uniforms, boots—and beer.

They had crossed almost the entire market when Esteban tugged at Malko's sleeve.

"That's him over there. The guy with the Kalashnikov."

She was pointing at a very dark-skinned old man with a short white beard. He wore a black turban whose ends fell on either side of his face. In demonstrating an AK-47 to a potential buyer, he suddenly aimed at the sky and fired a short burst.

"He's showing that it's in good working order," she said under her breath.

The Toubou and his customer continued talking and gesturing, and Malko and Esteban moved away. She seemed ill at ease.

"I think I'm going to leave you now," she said.

"How will you get back to the hotel?"

"I'll take a cab."

There were black-and-white taxis everywhere. Without waiting for Malko's answer, she disappeared.

He glanced at his watch. Night was falling, and the market

would soon close. The old Toubou was already starting to stack his pistols in a metal box.

Malko slipped into the crowd and walked back to the blue Ford.

"We're going to be following somebody," he told the CIA agent.

The American drove the car to the edge of the market, where the Toubou had almost finished packing up. He was carrying cardboard boxes to an old station wagon parked along Syria Street. Most of the other merchants were doing the same.

A quarter of an hour later, the Toubou slid behind the wheel and took off, accompanied by his helper, a small, equally dark-skinned boy. They turned into Syria Street and headed east, with the Ford following. It was already very dark, and there was no risk of the Toubou taking special notice of their car, which had Libyan plates. Besides, traffic was very heavy.

After a couple of miles, the station wagon turned into a small, dark street and pulled up in front of a low stone building. It was a nice enough neighborhood, with parked cars around.

The Toubou went inside, leaving the boy to lug the cartons into a ground-floor garage. Malko and the agent parked a little farther on and doused their headlights.

When the station wagon was empty, the boy went into the house in turn.

"What do we do now?" asked the agent.

"We wait."

The man inside had led Peter Farnborough to his death, so he must have a connection to Abu Bukatalla. They couldn't approach him in his home, of course, so they would have to wait for him to come out.

Malko turned to the American and said, "We may have to kidnap him."

"In that case, I'll need to talk to Ted."

"Go ahead and call him."

When he had the special-ops leader on the line, he handed Malko the phone.

"Ibrahim is okay," Ted announced right away. "And the bastards lost quite a few men."

"Did you capture Abu Bukatalla?"

"No."

"Were you able to follow them?"

"No, we weren't. Two of their pickups sacrificed themselves so they could get away."

Malko explained his situation. "This Toubou is our connection with Abu Bukatalla, and we have to make him talk," he said. "We can only do it on our own, so we'll have to question him 'at home.' "

Malko sensed reluctance, and Ted finally said:

"I have to get the green light from Cairo, though I think they'll give it to us. But it'll be a one-way street."

"What do you mean?"

"We can't turn the guy loose afterward. Too dangerous, politically. When you're finished with him, he's got to go."

Ted hung up.

In other words, if they kidnapped the old man, they would have to execute him. It wasn't Ted's decision, and enemy losses didn't concern him. He'd seen too many "bandits" killed in cold blood in Afghanistan and Iraq to be greatly troubled by the Toubou's fate.

This was war. In war, people die.

Malko looked at the building's gray facade and thought of

Jean-Paul Sartre's play *Dirty Hands*. In this business you sometimes had to get your hands dirty, give up part of your soul so as not to fail. It was a dilemma as old as the world.

Of course, if the Toubou stayed at home until morning, that would avoid the problem, because they couldn't stake out the house all night without being noticed.

Malko started when the CIA operative spoke:

"He's coming out."

It was true. The old man had emerged from the house and was heading for his car. He got in and took off, promptly followed by the blue Ford.

They drove for about twenty minutes, until they reached a wide avenue. The Toubou parked his station wagon among the other cars on a wide pullout across from the Venezia Café. He had barely stopped when a man stepped out of the shadows and joined him in his car. The two spent a few minutes together, then walked over to the big open-air restaurant. They took a table right below an enormous television screen showing a soccer match. They ordered nonalcoholic beer and were obviously going to have dinner.

"So what do we do now?" asked the American.

"We wait some more!"

It would be too risky for them to go sit in the restaurant, even though there were foreigners at a couple of the tables. The great majority of the clientele was Libyan, all men.

Adjoining the restaurant was its twin, reserved for families; a few women were eating there.

Malko pondered his next move. It would be tricky to continue following the Toubou; he might spot them. On the other hand, he was their only possible link to Abu Bukatalla. And Peter Farnborough had been brutally murdered because the man had warned the *takfiri* that the Englishman was on his trail.

Al-Senussi and Cynthia were sitting in the gloomy Ouzou dining room, eating in silence. Following the second attempt on his life, al-Senussi had come back to the hotel feeling deeply shaken. He now believed Cynthia's story about the attack on their plane, and he suspected there would be more attempts.

For her part, Cynthia was in the doldrums over her aborted rendezvous with Malko. He hadn't returned to the hotel, and the tiny Spanish woman was eating with some other NGO staffers at a table not far from theirs.

The Libyan broke the silence.

"Are you in contact with the leader of the Americans?" he asked.

"Yes, of course. Why?"

"I want you to go see them. I want to leave here, and not be part of their operation anymore. I'm very happy in London, I make a good living, and nobody tries to kill me. People here are too brutal."

Cynthia shot him a withering look. "Don't you want me to be the queen of Libya anymore?"

Al-Senussi ducked the question. "It's just that I don't want to die yet. This life isn't for me. I want you to ask your American friends to get me out of Benghazi as fast as possible."

"Tonight?"

"No, tomorrow morning. Tonight you're staying with me. Tell one of the security agents to drive you to where they are. I'm not setting foot outside the hotel. And tonight I need to relax."

He gave the young woman a burning look, and she understood what "relaxing" would involve.

Malko was still considering his options when the old man and his companion came out of the restaurant and headed for the station wagon. The Toubou took the wheel and drove along the side of the road, stopping near a small van a hundred yards farther on.

Malko and the agent followed on foot, lost in the crowd of restaurant customers returning to their cars.

They watched as some odd goings-on took place in the darkness. The unknown man opened the back of his van and pulled out a long package wrapped in cloth, which the Toubou immediately stowed in his station wagon. After three more such transfers, the man closed the van's doors.

Malko figured it out.

"That guy must be part of Abu Bukatalla's militia," he said. "He's selling weapons. The Toubou sold an AK-47 for him and must've given him the money."

The two men were now separating.

"Do we follow the militia guy?" asked the agent.

"No, it's too dangerous," he said. "Let's follow the Toubou."

"And do what?"

"We snatch him."

Malko had made up his mind. They absolutely had to find Abu Bukatalla, and they were running out of time.

Abu Bukatalla had established his headquarters in the desert near al-Abyar, a dozen miles east of Benghazi. Its site on a hill above the flat landscape gave him a clear view of any approaching adversaries. He'd sealed all but two of the openings in the walls around the farm and stocked the place with weapons and food, leaving the bulk of his matériel in a well-guarded warehouse in Derna.

Following the failure of his attack on al-Senussi, Abu Bukatalla sent out informants so he could plan a more targeted assault. It would have to be a surprise attack. Even he didn't have the strength to fight the Obeidi tribe, which had thousands of men under arms. And there was no more point in contacting the pretender to the Libyan throne.

Abu Bukatalla's second in command squatted next to him, an AK-47 close at hand, awaiting orders.

"Send somebody to the Ouzou Hotel," Abu Bukatalla said. "I want to know everything al-Senussi is up to, and especially anywhere he goes."

The *takfiri*'s idea was simple. Lacking an airplane, al-Senussi would have to leave Libya by road—a perfect opportunity for setting a trap.

As the militiaman left, another came in and handed Abu Bukatalla a wad of bills.

"Hisham says he has a customer for the guns I delivered," he said. "He'll let me know as soon as he has the money."

For Abu Bukatalla, trafficking in arms was a secondary source of income. True, Qatar gave him a lot of money, but it would be stupid not to turn the thousands of AK-47s stolen in Bayda into dinars. Once al-Senussi was killed, he would take a trip to Qatar to solidify his position. On that pleasant thought, he went to his tent and stretched out on a mattress on the ground.

The *takfiri* lived very frugally, eating dates, milk, and sometimes mutton, and drinking a great deal of tea. Like the Prophet.

The Toubou had just parked the station wagon across from his garage.

"Pull up closer," Malko told the operative.

The Toubou glanced at their car, probably assuming it was a neighbor coming home. He was carrying AK-47s when he found himself nose to nose with a blond foreigner who had stepped out of the blue car. He had eyes only for the pistol in the unknown man's right hand and stood paralyzed as Malko hissed an order:

"Get back in your car."

The old Toubou spoke enough English to understand. He put the weapons into the station wagon and slid behind the wheel. Malko got in beside him and pointed at the Ford.

"Follow that car."

The pistol jammed into his right side eliminated any temptation to argue. He started the car.

Malko stared at the Toubou's profile, repressing a powerful urge to put a couple of bullets in his head. After all, this was the man responsible for the savage murder of Peter Farnborough.

CHAPTER 23

The two cars passed through the entrance to the CIA base, whose gate immediately swung shut behind them.

The Toubou hadn't said a word during the whole drive, but Malko could see that his hands on the steering wheel were trembling. He was terrified. As they pulled up in front of the residence steps, Malko's cell rang. It was Ted.

"Stay in the car," he said. "We're coming to 'condition' him. Turn off the engine."

Malko switched off the ignition. The Toubou was staring straight ahead, hands clutching the wheel. Searchlights played on the lawn.

One of the rear doors opened and an agent slid in behind the Toubou, whipped off his glasses, and slapped a wide swath of black tape over his eyes, blindfolding him. Then he stepped out of the car, opened the driver's side door, and helped the Toubou out. In a flash, he tied his hands behind his back with plastic handcuffs, then led him into a garage next to the house. He sat him down and handcuffed him to a heavy metal chair.

The Toubou still hadn't said a word. Ted appeared and spoke to Malko in English:

"He's all yours."

For the first time, the old man opened his mouth and spoke.

Ted translated.

"He's asking why he was arrested. He wasn't doing anything wrong. He's a believer and he hates Qaddafi."

"Does he know Peter Farnborough?" Malko asked.

Ted put the question to him, then translated the answer.

"He says he doesn't know who that is."

"He's the man who asked him to lead him to Abu Bukatalla a few days ago," Malko said.

This time the Toubou nodded and spoke at length.

"Yes, he saw him but he doesn't know his name."

"What happened next?"

"He called Hassan, the man he knows in the militia, and passed on the foreigner's request. Hassan told him to set up a meeting for the next day in the militia's former barracks."

"And then?"

"The foreigner seemed very happy, he says, and gave him a hundred dinars. He hasn't seen him since."

The Toubou had clearly acted in good faith and had been manipulated. The MI6 agent, on the other hand, had been careless.

Now slumped with his head on his chest, the man wasn't faring very well.

"Can I go now?" he asked plaintively.

Ted answered with a few sharp words.

The prisoner immediately began to squirm in his chair and weep.

"I told him we're going to kill him," explained Ted, "because he's responsible for our friend's death."

To reinforce the threat, Ted took a Beretta 92 from under his shirt and inserted a magazine.

The blindfolded Toubou couldn't see him do it, but he recognized the characteristic click. Now he started to whimper like an unhappy puppy. Using his advantage, Ted pressed the gun's muzzle against the prisoner's neck.

The Toubou howled and shook his head, shrinking from the Beretta's steely pressure. Ted pulled the slide back, chambering a round.

This second click unleashed a new wave of cries and supplications from the Toubou.

"Tell him there is one way he can save his life," said Malko.

A brief dialogue followed, and Ted translated.

"He doesn't want to die. He has children, two wives, and he's a good Muslim. He'll do what we want."

"He has to take us to Abu Bukatalla."

This time the answer was even more tearful. Ted translated as he went along.

"He says that Abu Bukatalla is a very cruel man, very fanatical, a *takfiri*. If he does that, he will kill him, slit his throat like a sheep."

"Tell him that if he refuses, we'll kill him right now."

If the Toubou's hands had been free, he would have been wringing them. He was now moaning continuously. Ted said something to him, and his wails redoubled.

"What did you tell him?" asked Malko.

"That he had the right to pray one last time. That we're going to point him in the direction of Mecca."

As he spoke, Ted released the Toubou, who promptly fell to

his knees and started pounding his forehead against the concrete floor.

Malko and Ted exchanged a look: he was ripe.

"For the last time," Ted asked him, "where is Abu Bukatalla?"

"In the desert, in a farm out in the desert just before al-Abyar," he said. "There's only one road there."

"Is it far?"

"One hour away; the road is bad."

"You're going to take us there."

The Toubou banged his forehead on the concrete even harder.

"He says he doesn't want to," said Ted.

Malko didn't insist. They knew enough already. It would be easy enough to spot a camp of that size, even in the middle of the desert.

Overcome with gratitude, the Toubou now wouldn't stop talking. He explained that it was an abandoned farm with an oasis, in a hollow.

Ted made him shut up. They had all they needed.

"We'll take him down to the basement," he said. "We'll see if we can get more out of him tomorrow."

Ted had taken a couple of beers out of the fridge. He and Malko were sitting in the kitchen.

"So what do you want to do?" asked the American.

"You know Langley's instructions," answered Malko. "We have to eliminate Abu Bukatalla. That's an order from the White House. Without that, there won't be any Operation Sunrise."

Ted gave him a sideways glance.

"How are we supposed to do it?"

"You don't feel there are enough of you?"

Ted shook his head.

"I wouldn't try even if I had a written order from the SOG," he said. "We wouldn't stand a chance against those guys. They've got heavy weapons, they know how to fight, and they outnumber us twenty to one. Besides, a lot of those tangos fought in Iraq, and they hate us. They're prepared to embrace *shushala*"—martyrdom—"to take us down."

"You have any other ideas?"

Ted looked at him with a crooked grin.

"Sure: NATO. They've got the gear. Send in two F-16s and there'd be nothing left of the bastards. They'd never know what hit them. There's just one little snag. You'd have to convince NATO headquarters that they were a bunch of Qaddafists holed up in the desert. I don't have the balls to do that."

He took a swig of beer and slapped his bottle down.

The exchange left Malko feeling frustrated. Here they had figured where their enemy was hiding, but they couldn't hit him. The Americans had no organization in Libya—no attack drones and no ground troops, aside from a handful of Marines and CIA operatives.

"Okay, I'll talk it over with Jerry Tombstone tomorrow," he said. "By the way, do you have any news from the Ouzou?"

Ted smirked.

"Seems Ibrahim is working his girlfriend over so hard, our guys need earplugs. Lots of screaming, all night long. She must really want to be the queen of Libya."

"I'm not so sure about that," said Malko with a sigh.

Malko was lying on his bed, pondering his next move. He had thought of a way to bring all the necessary elements together for a counterpunch, but he lacked the main ingredient, a strike force.

Someone knocked gently on his door, and Malko shouted for whoever it was to come in. The young Chadian woman opened the door, then stepped aside to admit Cynthia.

Malko couldn't believe his eyes. Cynthia certainly didn't give up easily. But then he noticed she was wearing jeans and a high-collared blouse, hardly a seduction outfit. In any case, she quickly brought him down to earth.

"Ibrahim wants to leave!" she said. "He's in a rage and is threatening to drive off by himself if he doesn't get help."

In other words, throw himself into the clutches of Abu Bukatalla, who was almost certainly watching his movements.

"What's gotten into him?" asked Malko.

"He wants to drop everything. He's scared. They tried to kill him yesterday."

"I know. Where is he?"

"At the hotel."

"Okay, I'll go talk to him. Get yourself a cup of coffee. I'll be right there."

As soon as Malko was alone, he got dressed and ran out to the lawn with his Thuraya.

The CIA chief was flabbergasted.

"What is he thinking? Here we hand him a terrific deal on a silver platter, and he suddenly gets fussy."

"It's a silver platter all right, but with some lead in it. Ibrahim simply isn't the stuff of kings."

Tombstone was clearly dismayed.

"If I tell Washington this, they're going to kill me," he said with a groan. "They've put all their chips on him. You've got to bring him around."

"What if I'm not able to?"

"You'll manage," said Tombstone with his usual aplomb. "With Cynthia's help."

"There's another thing," Malko went on. "I've located Abu Bukatalla."

The CIA station chief hooted with joy.

"Fantastic! I want you to bring me that fucker's head."

"For the moment, I'd afraid I can't even give you a whisker from his beard," said Malko.

He explained the situation to Tombstone, who merely said:

"Well, you figure it out! We pay you a fortune to do that sort of thing, for Christ's sake. I'm sure the Agency pays you more than me."

"That's quite possible," said Malko, turning the knife in the wound. "But we don't run the same risks. Aside from cholera, yours are limited. But all right, I'll go try to buck up our future king."

In the Cherokee, Malko turned to Cynthia and said, "When Ibrahim sees me, I hope he doesn't start asking himself too many questions."

"He's so scared, he doesn't give a damn about anything," she said with a smile. "If we showed up hand in hand, he wouldn't even notice."

"From your mouth to God's ear!"

Just the same, Malko's heart was beating faster when they walked into the Ouzou. They didn't have to go far to find al-Senussi, who was sunk in one of the lobby's big leather armchairs. When he saw them, he popped up as if on a spring and ran over.

Cynthia introduced them, using her sweetest voice:

"Ibrahim, darling, I'd like you to meet Malko Linge, an Agency operative who is working to protect you."

The Libyan looked at him and frowned.

"Haven't I seen you somewhere before?"

"That's possible," said Malko easily. "I travel a lot."

Al-Senussi was still staring at him.

"Weren't you at the Four Seasons in Cairo?"

Malko wished the Earth would swallow him up. But he was on the spot and had to say, "That's right. I was already watching over you."

Al-Senussi didn't press the point.

"Okay, come back here," he said. "We have to talk."

They sat down across from the restaurant, and the Libyan cut right to the chase.

"I want you to tell your bosses that I'm giving up. I don't want to play the part they're asking me to."

"That's too bad," said Malko. "It's a grand adventure."

Al-Senussi nearly choked.

"They've already tried to kill me a couple of times!" he shouted. "I hate Libya!"

"But it's your country."

"This is the first time I've ever set foot here. I prefer London."

Malko didn't dare say that he shared his point of view. Instead he asked, "So what is it that you want?"

"To get out. Leave Benghazi. Drop everything."

"I'm not authorized to discuss your projects," said Malko.

"You can take that up with the people in London who got you into this business. But there's a problem: we don't have a flight to Cairo before the end of the week."

"In that case I'll go by road. I have money. I hear a taxi will take you, for a thousand dinars."

Malko was about to answer when he noticed a young bearded man on a nearby sofa who was eyeing them.

He leaned close to al-Senussi and said:

"Do you see the bearded man on the sofa there? I'm sure he's watching us, and he's almost certainly an Abu Bukatalla agent. Abu Bukatalla is just waiting to finish you off. And out on the highway, we can't do anything to protect you. It's eight hundred miles between Benghazi and Cairo."

Ibrahim al-Senussi's face fell.

"Then you have to find me a flight," he insisted. "For Cynthia, too."

He seemed to have regained his love of life.

Malko was about to reply when an idea suddenly occurred to him. It was an audacious plan and would be hard to carry out, but it would let him complete at least half his mission.

The most important half, in his eyes.

"Listen," he said. "Give me two or three days, and I'll arrange to get you exfiltrated."

"Is that so?"

"I swear it."

Malko's eyes met Cynthia's, and she immediately spoke up:

"You can believe him."

"Very well."

Ibrahim al-Senussi abruptly stood up and said, "Let me know when we can get under way."

He took Cynthia by the hand and led her to the elevator. Before he could pull her away, she gave Malko a long look that contained reproach—and many other things.

Al-Senussi had barely slammed the door to their room shut when he grabbed Cynthia by the throat and started banging her head against the wall.

"You slut!" he screamed, his eyes bulging. "You slept with that man! Do you think you're pulling the wool over my eyes?"

Afraid Ibrahim was going to kill her, Cynthia kicked at him, protesting:

"You're mad!" she yelled. "It isn't true!"

"Slut!" the Libyan repeated. "Don't you think I saw the way you were looking at him? If I hadn't been there, you would have laid down right on the floor. You're nothing but a whore!"

Al-Senussi's dark side was taking over.

A terrified Cynthia managed to jam her knee into his crotch, and he released her. She instantly bolted for the door and dashed out into the hallway. As she ran for the elevator, she yelled back at him, "Yes, it's true! He fucked me, and I hope he fucks me again!"

Abd al-Raziq received Malko promptly in his beautiful villa, which had been barely touched by the previous day's fighting.

Younes's nephew listened to him carefully, with growing interest.

"I can't take that kind of decision alone," the young man said. "Only the head of our tribe can do that, but I think he will listen to you."

"When?"

"I can take you to him right away, if you want."

"I'd like that," said Malko. "Time is short."

Al-Raziq left to make the arrangements, and Malko told himself that if God was on his side, Peter Farnborough would be avenged.

And there would be fewer *takfiri* in Libya.

CHAPTER 24

Ibrahim and Cynthia sat glaring at each other across one of the tables in the Ouzou's rear lounge. She was still breathless from running down four flights of stairs.

"You're coming up to the room," he snapped. "We have to talk."

"I bloody well won't! I don't want you killing me. Anyway, I didn't do anything. I just wanted to get back at you. That man doesn't mean a thing to me."

Al-Senussi, who wanted nothing better than to believe her, began to calm down.

"I believe you. But I don't want to hang around here. I'd rather go back to Cairo. Do you agree?"

That was certainly the only point on which the two of them saw eye to eye.

"Of course," she said.

"Okay then, I'm going to take care of the problem—without the Americans."

Al-Senussi went over to the front desk, whose somewhat

dimwitted Libyan clerk couldn't produce what he needed. He was about to give up when a smiling young man with a neatly trimmed beard approached him.

"Salaam alaikum. My name is Tarik. Are you looking for a taxi to Cairo?"

"Yes, I am. Why?"

"I have a car, a big Chrysler. I have already driven journalists to the front. My brother would accompany me because it's a long trip. It's best to have two drivers."

Al-Senussi couldn't believe his luck.

"How soon could we leave?"

"Inshallah, in a day or two. The car has to be serviced."

"How much are you charging?"

"Not much. It depends. How many of there are you?"

"Two people."

"Then it would be a thousand dinars. At the border, you have to buy special insurance for Egypt. It's somewhat expensive."

"That sounds fine," said al-Senussi. "Here's my number. Call me as soon as you're ready. And give me your number, too."

That done, he walked back over to Cynthia and explained the arrangements.

"But how do you know this Tarik person can be trusted?" she asked. "Malko said the road would be too dangerous. After everything that's happened, I'm not sure I want to go."

Dismayed at the idea of returning to Cairo without Cynthia, al-Senussi improvised quickly. He said, "I hinted at who I was, and I told him that powerful people had their eye on me. He seemed very impressed."

After all, it was almost true.

"And you're sure this is okay?" Cynthia asked again.

"We can leave in two days, at the most," he said.

The young woman abruptly relaxed. Some of her worries had just evaporated.

"Good for you!" she said, almost affectionately.

"Okay, we're going upstairs now."

This time, she followed him, even though she knew that Ibrahim would surely want to celebrate this good news with a party on her body.

That was a price she had to pay.

They had barely reached the room when al-Senussi stood her up against the wall, his body pressed to hers. She could feel his thick erection against her belly. She closed her eyes, thinking of Malko.

The old sheikh with the square beard was listening to Malko carefully. He wore a brown galabia and was leaning on cushions in a room that was bare except for a big flat-screen TV. A large map of eastern Libya lay in front of them, showing the various routes out of Benghazi.

Surrounded by the half dozen cousins who composed the Obeidi tribe's leadership, the sheikh had listened to Malko's suggestion, nodding.

He now broke the silence.

"Your idea is very appealing," he said approvingly. "Taking revenge on the men who savagely killed General Younes is our dearest wish. But the plan you have devised is complicated and hard to put into action."

"Why?" asked Malko.

"The idea of going through Ajdabiya and then taking the

highway to Tobruk is a good one. There's nothing but desert on either side of the road, and no towns along the way. But there's traffic in both directions, so there's no way to block the road with construction."

"Do you have any other ideas?" asked Malko.

"No, I don't," the sheikh admitted. "We'll have to think it over. Also, we need to know everything about their route, itinerary, and timetable. Otherwise this might all blow up in our faces."

The old Arab sipped his tea. Seeing Malko's obvious disappointment, he reassured him, "I will consult with the others and see how we can get what we need."

"We don't have much time," Malko reminded him.

The sheikh smiled to himself. "Allah alone is the master of time," he said.

He stood up, signaling the end of the meeting, and they embraced. Malko left the room in the company of Abd al-Raziq, who had brought him.

As they climbed into his Hyundai, the younger man spoke.

"Sheikh Obeidi is very cautious, but I'm sure he'll do everything he can to make your plan work. He won't rest until General Younes is avenged."

Those were encouraging words, but they weren't acts. Malko was on pins and needles. He had an excellent plan, but he sensed that a part of it was missing.

He had to find it, at any cost.

In the meantime, the old Toubou was still languishing in the Americans' basement. They couldn't keep him there forever. His family would worry about his disappearance and start asking questions.

Of course, they could just shoot him in the head and leave him somewhere out in the desert, as Ted had suggested.

Collateral damage.

But that solution revolted Malko, who wasn't a killer. Besides, the Toubou might still be useful.

When the Hyundai dropped him off, he still hadn't solved the problem.

Tarik could hardly contain himself, he was so eager to tell Abu Bukatalla that al-Senussi was hiring him for the trip to Cairo. He slowed down to pass through the narrow gate in the wall surrounding the farm where the militia had set up camp. From the outside, it just looked like an opening in the farm's enclosure. What you didn't see were the two guard posts hidden behind it, each equipped with a heavy machine gun to cut down any unwelcome visitors.

The moment he was through the gate, Tarik stopped. Two militiamen came over to inspect his vehicle and ask a few questions. Then one of them climbed in to accompany him to Abu Bukatalla.

The *takfiri* leader sat behind a desk in a roughly furnished room, with a few guards sitting on the ground.

Tarik was searched again. Even though he was a member of the militia himself, nobody was taking chances. In Libya, people were often turned, by money or other means.

When Abu Bukatalla was satisfied, he came to sit on the worn carpet next to the newcomer.

As Tarik gave him the good news, the Islamist thought he'd died and gone to heaven.

"Allah guided you!" he exulted. "Let's see which way you can drive them. Bring me a map."

A map was spread before them, and Abu Bukatalla pointed to it.

"You mustn't take the northern road, the one that goes through Derna," he explained. "There's a lot of traffic and checkpoints, and it's hard to get off it. You have to persuade your passengers to take the road that runs directly from Ajdabiya to Tobruk, through the desert. We can disappear easily there, once the job is done. Do you know if the Americans are going to accompany them?"

"No," Tarik admitted.

Abu Bukatalla waved that away.

"If they come, we'll kill them too, inshallah."

He took another look at the map. The road from Ajdabiya to Al'Adam and Tobruk was a straight shot 247 miles long, with only two towns along the way: Bir Tanjar and Bir Hakeim. The latter had been the site of one of the most ferocious battles of World War II, between the Afrika Korps and the French. Aside from that, there was nothing but flat, stony desert, with few roads on either side. An ideal place for an ambush.

The Islamist put his finger on the point along the route where a paved road from the north met the Ajdabiya-Tobruk highway.

"We could come down this road and wait for them along the way," he said. "We would then have more than a hundred and fifty miles to make our move."

He turned back to Tarik.

"Everything now depends on you, brother. You have to persuade them to go that way."

Tarik nodded.

"I'll do my best. I will need a big car—the Chrysler."

"That's no problem," said Abu Bukatalla. "Take the Chrysler. Your brother will accompany you. Plan to leave early in the morning, so as to be on the highway around nine o'clock."

Abu Bukatalla stood up and embraced him. Thanks to Tarik, he was going to accomplish what earlier had seemed impossible.

Cynthia was beaming.

"We're leaving the day after tomorrow at seven!" she announced.

Malko had run into the couple in the hotel lobby. The young woman looked radiant.

"Very well," he said. "I'll arrange an escort for you, at least while you're in Abu Bukatalla's zone of operations. Who is driving you?"

"A man here at the hotel offered to take us. He works with journalists, and he has a big car. He said the trip would take about fifteen hours, including crossing the Egyptian border. We'll save time by taking the direct Ajdabiya-Tobruk road; it's faster, apparently. Besides, it's out in the real desert. I like the desert."

There was no point in arguing.

Malko felt depressed. He hadn't been able to kill Abu Bukatalla, and Ibrahim al-Senussi's dreams of royalty were up in smoke.

There was nothing left for him to do in Benghazi.

"Can I come with you as far as Cairo?" he asked.

Before al-Senussi could open his mouth, Cynthia said, "Of course!"

"I'll alert my American friends," said Malko. "I'll be here at six thirty, day after tomorrow."

Driving to the CIA base, he had a bitter taste in his mouth.

Though smiling when he greeted him, Ted frowned when he heard Malko's plans.

"I'd be careful," he said. "There aren't many people on the Ajdabiya-Tobruk road. If you have car trouble, it could be a hassle. We'll give you a couple of Cherokees and accompany you as far as we can. But are you really sure you want to leave?"

"There's nothing left for me to do here," said Malko.

"Suit yourself. What do we do with the guy in the basement?"

Malko had completely forgotten about the old Toubou. He knew that Ted considered him as good as dead, but Malko hated to see him killed. After all, he was just a small-time trafficker who hadn't done them any harm. Suddenly he had an idea.

"Lend him to me in a little while."

"What for?"

"I want to ask him something, show him someone. It's a long shot."

"No problem."

Malko had parked the Ford on the Urubah Road median just before the turnoff to the Ouzou Hotel.

The weary Toubou was seated beside him, in handcuffs. Ted and a Marine were in the back.

As they watched, a big blue car slowed to take the turnoff.

"Here we go!" Malko told the Toubou. "Take a good look at that car and the people in it."

It was the Chrysler that would take al-Senussi to Cairo; the Libyan had made an appointment to inspect it beforehand.

The driver of the Chrysler chatted with the rebels at the checkpoint under their "national" umbrella, and one of them raised the barrier to let him drive up to the hotel. The car stopped at the entrance and a man stepped out.

The Toubou turned toward the backseat and said a few words in Arabic.

"He says he knows that man," Ted translated. "He belongs to Abu Bukatalla's militia."

Malko suddenly recognized him, too. He was the man the old Toubou had handed money to in front of the Venezia Café.

The link was established. Malko had just gotten the proof of what he'd suspected, that Abu Bukatalla was setting a trap for Ibrahim al-Senussi.

"Let's go," he said. "We're going home."

Al-Senussi was relaxing in his room with Cynthia. The Ouzou didn't have a pool or anywhere nice to hang out, and there was nothing to do in town. Just then, the phone rang. It was the front desk. The man called Tarik was asking for him.

"I'll be right down," said the Libyan.

He'd asked the driver to show him the car that would take them to Cairo, to make sure it wasn't a piece of junk.

A smiling Tarik awaited him at the front desk.

"The car is outside," he said.

Al-Senussi followed him. A big blue Chrysler was parked in front of the hotel steps, with another man at the wheel. Tarik introduced him:

"This is my brother; he's coming with us. The car is in his name."

Al-Senussi inspected the Chrysler, which seemed to be in good shape, though he was startled to see that it had seventy thousand miles on the odometer.

"It's been very well maintained," said Tarik, "and we have two spare tires. The AC works."

That was the least you could expect.

Satisfied, al-Senussi confirmed their departure.

"Be here at seven o'clock sharp. There will be three of us. A friend is coming along."

Tarik nodded, unperturbed, and drove away.

As he had the last time, Abd al-Raziq drove Malko to the tribe's headquarters. Malko had to wait for a while, because the sheikh was in a meeting. Then, over the ritual tea, the old man asked:

"Do you have any news?"

"Yes," said Malko. "I now know when al-Senussi is leaving, I know his itinerary, and I have the proof that Abu Bukatalla will try to kill him."

The sheikh of the Obeidi listened to his explanation carefully. He then launched into a long speech in Arabic, translating Malko's information for his neighbors, which took quite some time. After a lively discussion, the old sheikh spoke to him again, in English.

"This changes everything," he said. "We had been thinking of how to proceed but lacked some elements. It now seems possible. Here's what we're going to do."

Listening closely, Malko liked what he heard.

"Your plan is perfect," he said.

"It can fail, of course, and in that case our friend will lose his life, but this is our only option."

"I'll lose mine as well," Malko pointed out. "I'm riding with them."

The sheikh remained impassive.

"You're a brave man," he said. "We have just enough time to get everything ready. Inshallah, we may meet again. Otherwise . . ."

Malko stretched out his hand.

"No matter, so long as the plan works."

If it did, he would have squared the circle.

Malko was neither hungry nor sleepy. In a few hours he would know if his double-or-nothing gamble was going to pan out.

If it didn't, he would be dead, something he'd always anticipated, though without desiring it. At least nobody could criticize him for not trying.

The old Toubou was again locked up in the base's garage. Malko made Ted promise to release him the next day, after threatening him enough to keep him from talking.

Anyway, he didn't know that much.

It had been daylight for a long time, and the Ouzou's breakfast room was crowded when Malko joined Ibrahim and Cynthia there. The young woman was wearing tight jeans, boots, and a fitted green blouse. She was made up as if she were going to a party.

Malko had an execrable cup of coffee with them.

Al-Senussi was nervous.

"What's keeping him?" he grumbled.

He'd no sooner said that when Tarik appeared, smiling and polite. The driver declined their offer of a cup of coffee.

"The car is ready," he announced. "I had your bags loaded. We can leave whenever you like."

They were already on their feet.

The blue Chrysler was parked in front of the hotel steps, along with two unmarked white Cherokees—the CIA escort.

Tarik didn't seem to pay them any attention, and Malko explained:

"They will escort us as far as the Ajdabiya turnoff."

A few minutes later the little convoy took off under the indifferent gaze of an elegant, almost aristocratically thin cat sprawled on the hotel steps.

They started on the Urubah Road toward the Brega–Ra's Lanuf highway. There was a lot of traffic, and they couldn't drive very fast. Beyond the last checkpoint, the highway ran straight and they sped up, passing the Qaddafi army's wrecked armored column—including the self-propelled howitzer that had earlier sheltered Malko and Cynthia.

Malko sat in front beside the driver. Cynthia and Ibrahim were in the rear, and the second driver was behind them.

Nobody talked. Ibrahim held Cynthia's hand.

Behind his dark glasses, Malko was studying the landscape, though he knew they weren't in the danger zone yet. Many heavily armed pickups were on the highway, heading in both directions.

An hour and a half later, the houses became denser as the highway entered Ajdabiya.

Tarik slowed down. Though there wasn't any sign, he took the correct turnoff for the highway east, which passed by a busy gas station. Beyond it, there was nothing for the next 250 miles.

Just then, Malko heard honking behind them. An arm waved from the lead Cherokee.

The Americans were saying good-bye.

The two SUVs made a U-turn, and Malko watched in the rearview mirror as they disappeared. Now they were alone. Ibrahim and Cynthia thought they were driving home, unaware that they might be heading to their deaths. Malko had a Beretta 92 in his briefcase, a gift from Ted.

It wasn't much.

Tarik accelerated on a road that stretched straight ahead without a turn for hundreds of miles. They encountered few vehicles. Desert to the left, desert to the right, and some hazy uplands in the distance: the Mintaqat Umm Qihuwari range. Like most of Libya, the area was completely empty and inhospitable.

The highway looked as if it were buckling under the sun.

Malko mentally calculated the distance as they covered it. After an hour he noticed a track leading off into the desert on their left. It was probably the Saurinu road. He tensed. If there was going to be trouble, it would be around here.

Nothing happened until he noticed a cloud of dust behind them on their right.

His heart began to beat faster.

The dust cloud shrank and Malko could make out vehicles that had turned off the track onto the paved highway.

It was almost certainly Abu Bukatalla's armada, which was now after them. Cynthia and Ibrahim hadn't noticed anything.

Suddenly a tanker truck appeared in the middle of the road

ahead of them, forcing Tarik to slow to about forty miles an hour.

Malko turned around. He could now identify the vehicles following them: a column of pickups.

In front of them, the tanker truck was still driving quite slowly, and Tarik began furiously honking his horn. The pickups were getting closer.

When the column was no more than a hundred yards behind it, the tanker truck finally pulled over. Tarik shot by him, honking furiously, but then, oddly enough, didn't speed up. It was as if he'd gone to sleep.

Malko was as tight as a violin string.

He looked in the rearview mirror. If he saw the front bumper of even one pickup passing the tanker truck, his life would soon be over.

Abu Bukatalla gazed at the highway, his folding AK-47 across his knees. He thanked Allah for his great gift. He was going to kill not only Ibrahim al-Senussi, but a CIA agent in the bargain.

He couldn't have hoped for anything more.

His eight pickups drove in the middle of the highway, preventing other vehicles from passing them.

Suddenly they found themselves behind a tanker truck. Abu Bukatalla's driver honked, but the truck didn't move aside.

"The dog!" muttered Abu Bukatalla.

Now, as they drove a few dozen yards behind the truck, an unexpected smell suddenly reached his nostrils. It took him a few moments to realize that it was gasoline. He turned to his driver and asked:

"Do we have a leak?"

But he immediately realized his mistake. All his pickup trucks ran on diesel.

The pavement in front of him seemed strangely wet. But before he had time to wonder why, he caught sight of a pickup parked beside the road with a man standing next to it.

As his pickup passed them, the man raised his arm and threw something onto the highway, then immediately dropped to the ground.

"*Stop!*" Abu Bukatalla screamed.

But it was too late: the entire convoy was suddenly surrounded by a sea of flames.

A stretch of highway more than a hundred yards long was burning. Orange and red flames rose around the pickups.

Abu Bukatalla saw the fire licking the sides of his pickup.

His driver, who didn't know what else to do, unwisely hit the brakes, and flames immediately engulfed the vehicle.

Its paint and fuel caught fire, and black smoke darkened the windshield.

Abu Bukatalla threw the door open and jumped out, immediately becoming a human torch.

The flames from the gasoline that the tanker truck had sprayed on the highway were burning everything, stopping the column in its tracks. Some of the pickups' ammunition began to explode. Men tried to flee, engulfed in flames.

By now the tanker truck was far away, almost out of sight.

Rising from the road was a huge cloud of black smoke that could be seen for miles.

Sheikh Obeidi drove along the column of blazing pickups, at a safe distance from the fire, his twin 23 mm cannons systematically raking the paralyzed vehicles and their occupants. He yelled:

"La illah illa Allah!"

Vengeance was sweet.

His magazines empty, he stopped. Once the guns were reloaded, he took another pass by the column going in the other direction, but there was no need. Abu Bukatalla's militiamen were all dead, either shot or burned to death.

As he drove by, the Obeidi man who had thrown the incendiary grenade to ignite the sprayed gasoline gave him a joyous wave.

They had wasted several hundred gallons of gasoline, but the result was well worth it. In an irony of fate, the gasoline had just been delivered by a tanker from Abu Bukatalla's ally, Qatar.

Malko felt as relaxed as if he'd just had a good massage. Behind him, the column of smoke continued to rise into the sky.

Clutching the steering wheel, Tarik stubbornly stared straight ahead.

"You okay, Tarik?" asked Malko teasingly.

The driver didn't answer, merely nodded.

Cynthia had turned around and was looking back.

"What's that behind us?" she asked.

"Must be an accident," said Malko calmly.

He would have plenty of time to tell her about it, later. They exchanged a long look, and Malko realized that he was now in a hurry to get to Cairo.

About the Translator

William Rodarmor (1942–) is a veteran French literary translator in Berkeley, California. He recently translated *The Last King of the Jews*, by Jean-Claude Lattès (Open Road, 2014) and *The Yellow Eyes of Crocodiles*, by Katherine Pancol (Penguin, 2013), and was a fellow at the Banff International Literary Translation Centre. He served as a Russian linguist in the Army Security Agency and worked as a French interpreter for the U.S. State Department.